"No," she breathed out on a gasp of shock. "Not you."

Imogene barely heard the groan of "Not again" that came from the groom's side of the room. Instead, her gaze was fixed on the man who'd finally turned to face her.

Valentin Horvath.

The man she'd divorced seven years ago.

Imogene stood rooted to the spot, staring at the man she'd shared more intimacies with than any other human being in existence. The man who had not only broken her heart but crushed it so completely that it had taken her all this time to even contemplate marriage again.

And yet, beneath the anger, beneath the implacable surety that there was no way this marriage could go ahead, came that all-too-familiar flicker of sexual recognition that had led to their first hasty, fiery and oh-so-short union.

* * *

Inconveniently Wed is part of the Marriage at First Sight series from *USA TODAY* bestselling author Yvonne Lindsay.

Dear Reader,

Welcome to *Inconveniently Wed*, book two in my Marriage at First Sight series. Have you ever wondered about the one who got away? A partner who may have swept you off your feet but then circumstances changed and your relationship never went any further? And what if they were Mr. or Ms. Right all along? Could you imagine a second chance? Would you take it?

The reunion, quite literally, of Valentin Horvath and his estranged wife, Imogene, is difficult and fraught with bitterness from their combined pasts. So much water lies under the vast bridge that stretches between them, it's hard to imagine that they're ever going to make it. And then there's the matter of the woman who drove them apart in the first place. Can they make this marriage for keeps and risk their hearts all over again, or will history simply repeat itself?

I hope you enjoy reading *Inconveniently Wed*. I'd love to hear what you think of Valentin and Imogene's story. Feel free to contact me via my website, www.yvonnelindsay.com, or through Facebook, at www.Facebook.com/yvonnelindsayauthor.

Happy reading!

Yvonne Lindsay

YVONNE LINDSAY

INCONVENIENTLY WED

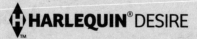

Recycling programs
for this product may
not exist in your area.

ISBN-13: 978-1-335-60341-8

Inconveniently Wed

This edition published by arrangement with Harlequin Books S.A.

For questions and comments about the quality of this book, please contact us at CustomerService@Harlequin.com.

® and TM are trademarks of Harlequin Enterprises Limited or its corporate affiliates. Trademarks indicated with ® are registered in the United States Patent and Trademark Office, the Canadian Intellectual Property Office and in other countries.

Printed in U.S.A.

Award-winning *USA TODAY* bestselling author **Yvonne Lindsay** has always preferred the stories in her head to the real world. Married to her blind-date sweetheart and with two adult children, she spends her days crafting the stories of her heart. In her spare time she can be found with her nose firmly in someone else's book.

Books by Yvonne Lindsay

Harlequin Desire

Wed at Any Price

Honor-Bound Groom
Stand-In Bride's Seduction
For the Sake of the Secret Child

Courtesan Brides

Arranged Marriage, Bedroom Secrets
Contract Wedding, Expectant Bride

Marriage at First Sight

Tangled Vows
Inconveniently Wed

Visit her Author Profile page at Harlequin.com, or yvonnelindsay.com, for more titles.

I wouldn't be here without my wonderful readers, so this story is for you. Thank you for all your support and kind words through the years.

One

"It's going to be okay, Mom." Imogene hastened to reassure her mother for the thousandth time.

She had no doubt her mom remembered all too well the broken woman Imogene had been when she'd returned from volunteering in Africa with her first marriage and all her hopes and dreams in tatters. But as she'd told her mom several times, things were going to be completely different this time around. This marriage would be based on mutual compatibility after an intense clinical assessment by a team of relationship counselors and psychologists—absolutely nothing impractical about that. She'd done the passionate love thing. Experienced the soaring highs of love at first sight and barely made it through the devastating

lows of discovering it had all been a lie. This way, at least, nothing would go wrong.

"Ready?" the wedding planner asked in her perfectly calming and well-modulated voice.

Imogene smoothed a hand down her gown, the silk-and-organza creation a far cry from the borrowed cocktail dress she'd worn to her last wedding, and nodded. "Absolutely."

The wedding planner gave her a wide smile, then indicated to the pianist to change his music for the bride's entrance. Imogene hesitated at the door. Then, taking her mother's hand, she began to walk slowly and confidently toward the man she was going to build a future and create a much-longed-for family with. A serene smile wreathed her face as she briefly made eye contact with her friends and the sprinkling of extended family who'd made the trip to the West Coast from New York. The formality of signing the license application could be done separately here in Washington, which kept to the Match Made in Marriage rules of meeting at the altar. This was the right thing for an old-fashioned girl with old-fashioned values to do, she assured herself. This time she wasn't leaving anything to chance. This time, she was getting it right.

The last time Imogene had married, she'd been filled with excitement together with a crazy-mad dose of lust. *And look how that turned out*, the little voice inside her head reminded her. She grimaced slightly. Today was different. There was no bubbling

excitement, beyond a quiet curiosity as to exactly what her groom would be like, and there was certainly no lust. At least not yet.

No, this time she was not a victim of the dizzying heights of passion—a passion that had blurred her sensibilities, not to mention her common sense. This time she had a specific goal in mind. A family of her own. Yes, she knew she could take steps to be a parent by herself, but she didn't want to do it alone. She truly wanted a like-minded companion. Someone she could grow to love over time. Someone with whom she could be sure that love would have longevity, if only because of the time it took to grow. And if love didn't come? Could she live without it? Of course she could. She'd done the impulsive marriage before, and it had left her shattered when it all fell apart. This time she'd taken every precaution to ensure there would be none of that. With care and mutual respect, anything was possible.

But was marrying at first sight taking things a step too far? Her parents obviously thought so. Her father hadn't even come to Port Ludlow, here in Washington, for the ceremony, citing an important human rights case he was working on. But his distaste for her entering into an agreement with the exclusive matchmaking agency, which discreetly boasted a 100 percent success rate, had been clear. To him the very prospect of meeting your husband or wife at the altar was a recipe for disaster, but the dictates of Match Made in Marriage were clear. There was no chance

to meet your intended prior to the ceremony and both participants had to put their trust completely in the matchmaking process. Imogene took a quick look at her mom, who had agreed to accompany her only daughter down the aisle to marry a stranger. Caroline O'Connor looked back, her gaze meeting and melding with her daughter's—concern for what Imogene was doing clearly reflected there.

Her eyes were glued to her groom waiting at the altar with his back turned, a man whose posture showed he was the kind of person used to being in command. A frisson of awareness tickled at the back of her neck. As they neared the front row, her mom hesitated and bestowed a swift kiss on Imogene's cheek before taking her seat. Imogene took a deep breath and focused anew on the stranger standing there. Waiting for her. There was something about the set of his shoulders and the shape of his head that prodded at her memory. Something that wasn't right.

As he turned around, disbelief flooded every cell in her body and she stopped a few feet from the altar.

Recognition dawned.

"No," she breathed out in shock. "Not you."

Imogene barely heard the groan of "Not again" that came from the groom's side of the room. Instead, her gaze was fixed on the man who'd finally turned to face her.

Valentin Horvath.

The man she'd divorced seven years ago.

There should have been some satisfaction that his expression was equally as stunned as her own must be, but there was none. In fact, satisfaction took a back seat while anger and confusion vied for supremacy. Imogene stood rooted to the spot, staring at the man she'd shared more intimacies with than any other human being in existence. The man who had not only broken her heart, but crushed it so completely that it had taken her all this time to even contemplate marriage again.

And yet, beneath the anger, beneath the implacable certainty that there was no way this marriage could go ahead, was that all-too-familiar flicker of sexual recognition that had led to their first hasty, fiery and oh-so-short union. Imogene did her best to quell the sensations that bloomed to life inside her traitorous body, to ignore the sudden flush of heat that simmered from deep inside and radiated outward. To pay no heed to the way her nipples had grown tight and hypersensitive in the French lace bustier she wore beneath her strapless gown. It was merely a physiological response to a healthy male, she told herself. It meant nothing.

He meant nothing.

Valentin reached a hand toward her.

"No," she repeated. "This is not happening."

"I couldn't agree more," said her ex-husband very firmly. "Let's get out of here."

He took her by the elbow and she reluctantly allowed him to lead her toward a side room—all the

while fighting to disregard the realization that they might have been apart all these years but the fire that always burned so fiercely between them had reignited just like that. Her skin warmed where his hand lightly cupped her elbow, her senses keenly attuned to the size of him, to the heat that emanated from his large form, to the scent he still wore. A scent that she'd tried her hardest to forget but that seemed to be indelibly imprinted on her limbic system.

An older woman with a cloud of silver hair and alert blue eyes rose from her seat in the front row of the groom's side of the room.

"Valentin?"

"Nagy," he said in acknowledgment. "I think you need to come with us. You have some explaining to do."

Some explaining to do? Imogene's brow creased in ever-growing confusion. She recognized the diminutive of the Hungarian word for *grandmother* from back when Valentin used to talk about his family. But how could his grandmother have anything to do with this?

"Yes, I believe I do," replied the old woman in a firm voice. She turned to appease the assembled guests with a reassuring smile. "Don't worry, everyone, we'll be back shortly."

Back shortly? Imogene doubted that very much, but she allowed Valentin to guide her along in his grandmother's wake as she walked purposefully ahead of them.

* * *

"Explain yourself," Valentin demanded, rounding on his grandmother the moment she closed the door behind them.

"I did exactly what you asked me to do. I found you a wife."

"I don't understand," Imogene interjected.

Valentin didn't understand, either. The brief he'd given Alice had been pretty straightforward. He wanted a wife and he wanted a family. After his first failed attempt seven years ago, when he'd thrown his usual logic to the four corners of the world and leaped before looking, he'd decided to take a more rational approach. He did not—in any way, shape or form—expect to see his ex-wife approach him here today. No matter how much more beautiful she'd grown in the years since he'd last seen her.

He took a moment to fill his gaze with the vision of loveliness that was his ex. She hadn't changed that much. Not her dark auburn hair that so richly adorned her head or her green-gray eyes that snapped angrily at him now or her smooth alabaster skin that had always shown every mark from his five o'clock shadow—making it necessary for him to shave twice a day when they were together. He'd have done anything for her, once—shaving twice a day was the least of it. But all that was in the past, and would remain there.

He transferred his attention to his grandmother,

who composed herself with her usual grace and instinctive air of command before speaking.

"Imogene, let me explain a little. But first, please, take a seat. And, Valentin, that means you, too. You know I can't tolerate your pacing. You always did have ants in your pants, even as a child."

Valentin bit back the retort that in this case, he had every right to pace. Instead, he gestured to Imogene to take a chair in the small side office and took another for himself. They were close enough that he could smell her fragrance. It was something different from what she used to wear but no less potent when it came to his senses. He used his customarily rigid control to ignore the way the scent teased at him, inviting him to lean a little nearer, to inhale more deeply, and instead focused on watching his grandmother.

Alice settled herself behind the desk and rested her age-spotted hands on the blotter in front of her. She took her time to speak, obviously choosing her words carefully.

"I would like to remind you both that you have signed a contract to marry today."

"Not him!"

"Not her!"

Their responses were simultaneous and equally emphatic.

"I don't recall either of you stating any exclusions when you approached Match Made in Marriage. Do you?" She arched one silver brow and gave them each a pointed look. "No, of course not. Because when you

signed the contracts with Match Made in Marriage, you gave us an undertaking to find you your ideal life partner. Which I—" she hesitated and corrected herself "—*we* did."

"What?" Imogene gasped and turned her gaze on Valentin. "Your grandmother is a part of all this?"

He nodded. "She is. And she's usually very good at it, but in our case, she's clearly made a mistake."

Alice sighed and rolled her eyes. "I do not make mistakes, Valentin. Never, and especially not in this case."

"You can't seriously begin to expect me to believe that," he responded, his voice rising in frustration. "We ended our marriage seven years ago due to irreconcilable differences."

"Infidelity," Imogene injected into the conversation. "Yours."

Valentin held on to his temper by a thread. "As I said, irreconcilable differences. As far as I am aware nothing else has changed between us, so I fail to see how Imogene became my perfect match. Your instincts have failed you this time."

"Instincts?" Imogene's voice ran cold. "I was of the understanding matches are made using specialists, not mumbo jumbo. Doesn't that put *you* in breach of contract, Mrs. Horvath?"

Valentin watched his grandmother level a considering look at his ex-wife.

"You will find that the 'mumbo jumbo' as you so dismissively call it is well-defined under clause 24.2.9

subparagraph *a*. I believe the term has been set out as 'subjective assessment by Match Made in Marriage.'"

"That's ridiculous," Imogene protested.

"May I remind you that no one forced you to sign the contract," Alice said in a voice that dripped icicles.

"Either way," Valentin interrupted before Imogene could let fly a volley of words that he imagined were hovering on the edge of her tongue, "what you have done is gross manipulation of us both. This doesn't need to become uncivil. Contracts can be broken. I think I speak for both Imogene and myself when I say this marriage will go not ahead."

"And I speak for Match Made in Marriage when I say it definitely will. You are right for each other."

"Impossible!" Imogene snorted inelegantly. "I specifically said that infidelity was a deal breaker. If my prospective partner could not promise to remain faithful to me, I could not contemplate marriage with him. What about that was not clear?"

"I was not unfaithful," Valentin protested in frustration.

They'd gone over this already seven years ago. But Imogene's refusal to accept his word, and his promise to her, had seen her walk out on him without so much as a backward glance. In fact, for her, at least, it had been all too easy to call an end to their life together. To the dreams they'd shared, let alone the passion. Still, he'd reminded himself often in those early days, it was better he'd found out her

lack of staying power then, rather than later when there may have been children to consider, as well.

"Stop behaving like a pair of squabbling children!" Alice admonished them both. "Your pairing was ascertained after rigorous testing. There is no one else more perfect for each of you than each other. Now, Valentin, do you trust me?"

"I'm not so sure about that anymore, to be completely honest with you, Nagy." He rubbed a hand over his jaw.

"Well, that's regrettable," Alice said on a sniff of disapproval. "But perhaps you will realize the error of your ways. You can have a successful marriage despite how unfortunately your last attempt at being a couple ended."

"A-attempt?" Imogene spluttered. "You say that as if I made the decision to leave Valentin lightly, when I can assure you I did not."

Alice waved a slender hand in the air as if Imogene's words were of no consequence. "The facts here today remain that you each requested a life partner when you contracted Match Made in Marriage. All the data gleaned during your screening process supports my—*our*—decision to match you. I'm aware you two have issues—"

"I-issues?" It was Valentin's turn to splutter now.

"Hear me out, please," Alice commanded with a quelling glare at him. "Can you both honestly say that seeing each other again leaves you totally cold?"

Valentin shifted a little in his chair, all too aware

that his physical reaction to Imogene when he'd seen her today had been as fierce and as instant as it had ever been. He still remembered the first time he'd met her, when she'd brought a child from her primary school into the ER where he was a trauma specialist. Even as he'd switched into his clinician's role seamlessly, he hadn't remained unmoved by her presence. Now, with her seated beside him, studiously avoiding his gaze when he turned to look at her again, he observed the proud posture of her slender body and the surprisingly determined line of her jaw. A jaw he'd traced with kisses. His body clenched on a surge of desire—his instinctive need for her as overwhelming as it had ever been—and he turned his stare back to his grandmother.

"No, I cannot," he said with great reluctance.

"And, Imogene? When you realized it was Valentin waiting at the altar for you today? How did you feel when you saw him?"

"Confused," she said bluntly.

"And?" Alice prompted.

"Fine, I was attracted to him. But attraction isn't the only thing necessary to make a marriage work. We proved that already."

"Yes, you did," Alice conceded. "But since that attraction still burns between you, don't you think you owe it to yourselves to find out if, under different circumstances from those in which you originally met, you can make an honest attempt at a good marriage?"

"I believed I was making more than an attempt at

the time," Imogene protested. "I loved Valentin with all my heart. A heart he subsequently broke."

Alice sighed and leaned back in her chair, settling her hands in a loose clasp in her lap. "I see," she acknowledged. "And it still hurts, doesn't it?"

Imogene gave Alice a stiff nod.

"Then you still have unresolved feelings for my grandson, don't you?"

Valentin made a sound of protest. "Nagy, that's not fair. She made her decision a long time ago. You can't make us do this. It's cruel and unnecessary."

"It's never easy facing your failures," Alice said, slowly and stiffly rising from her seat. "I will leave you two for a few minutes to discuss this further. I strongly urge you to give your marriage one more chance. Your circumstances have changed dramatically since then. Neither of you is as young or as volatile as you were and, I might point out, neither of you has found a more suitable mate since. Please, discuss this as rational adults. Be certain that you won't spend the rest of your lives wondering if you should have given each other another chance. I will wait outside for your decision. Don't make me wait too long."

Two

The door closed as Alice left them alone in the room.

"She's a piece of work, your grandmother," Imogene said harshly. "How dare she do this?"

"She dares because it's what she does."

Imogene rose from her chair, her gown whispering with her rapid movement and her breasts heaving above the jeweled neckline.

"What she does? Seriously? You're condoning her behavior?" Imogene forced a short laugh from her throat. It was either that or scream.

"No, I'm not condoning it. I'm as angry and as shocked as you are. I never thought in a million years..."

She stared at Valentin as he rose to his feet and

faced her. Always a big man, he dwarfed the room, but she wasn't scared of him. She knew all too well how gentle he could be—how tender his touch was. Her pulse kicked up a beat and she fiercely quelled the direction of her thoughts. This wasn't what she'd signed up for.

"A million years wouldn't be long enough," she murmured, and turned her face from his piercing blue-eyed gaze.

No, she thought. The end of time wouldn't be long enough to undo the ravages of their first union. He'd taken her love, her adoration, her heart. Then he'd thrown it all away. She'd never forget that moment she'd walked into their small house and smelled the distinctive heady perfume one of his colleagues at the hospital had always worn. Nor would she forget walking on legs that had become stiff and wooden toward the bedroom where she'd discovered said colleague, still naked and drowsy in her and Valentin's bed.

The sheets of the bed had been tumbled in disarray. The combined scents of fresh sweat and sex had been heavy on the air. Imogene had heard the sound of the shower running in the tiny bathroom down the hall but she hadn't waited to see her husband. When his colleague Carla had asked if she was looking for Valentin and gestured to the bathroom, she'd turned on her heel and marched straight back through town and stopped at the first law office she'd seen.

Numbly she'd gone through the motions of filing

to dissolve the marriage that had obviously meant so little to Valentin and yet had meant the world to her. *He* had meant the world to her. Until she'd been faced with his infidelity.

She'd been in such a state of shock. Was it possible she'd misunderstood Carla? But then again, if she had, why had Valentin so easily given her up? If he was as innocent as he protested himself to be, why—at any time in the next few weeks—didn't he find her at the hotel she moved her things into until she could be released from her teaching contract and get the next flight back to the States? Instead, he'd simply let her go, which smacked of a guilty conscience to her—both then and now. Besides, she didn't want to think for a minute that she'd made a mistake, or that she'd behaved rashly in the heat of the moment. Carla had had no reason to lie, and Imogene knew the other woman and Valentin had been an item before her own arrival in Africa. Valentin himself had told her. More fool her, she'd believed him when he'd said it was over—that Imogene was the only woman for him.

She was dragged back into the present by the sound of Valentin clearing his throat.

"So I'm guessing you're a no, then?"

"You're guessing right," she answered adamantly.

"Not even prepared to think about it?" he coaxed.

"Not even," she said firmly. "I will not marry a philanderer ever again."

"Imogene." He said her name softly, with a tone of regret lacing the three syllables together in a way

that struck her at her core. "I was never unfaithful to you."

"I know what I saw, Valentin. Don't take me for a complete idiot."

He shoved a hand through his hair in a gesture of frustration. "What you saw was—"

"Your mistress, curled up in my sheets, in my bed, and stinking of you!" she answered viciously.

"It wasn't what you thought it was."

"Oh, so now you're going to tell me you never slept with her?"

"You know I can't tell you that, but I told you the truth when I said that had all been in the past. I was never unfaithful to you," he affirmed.

"You say one thing. I saw another."

Valentin took a step toward her and she took a step back, but her motion was halted by the wall behind her. She looked up at him, her nostrils flaring, her mouth drying as she studied his oh-so-familiar features. Involuntarily, she stared at the lines that had deepened around his eyes, the new ones on his forehead, the stubble that persistently made its presence felt even though he would have shaved only a short time ago. His face had been so dear to her once. If she closed her eyes now she could recall every aspect of it—the color of his eyes in exquisite detail, the short dark lashes that intently framed those eyes, the way that special shade of blue darkened and deepened when he was aroused. The way they were doing now.

A bolt of desire hit her. There had never been any

other man who had this effect on her. Ever. Only Valentin. No one had ever come close to him, nor, she admitted ruefully, would again. Which left her between the devil and the deep blue sea, didn't it? Go against everything she'd promised herself she would never accept, or settle for less than what she knew Valentin could give her.

"Can we call a truce?" Valentin asked, his voice husky.

She knew that sound, knew he was gripped by the same intense need for her that she suffered for him. But in her case it was only for him. Could he say the same? She doubted it.

"Maybe," she answered reluctantly.

"What brought you here today?" he asked.

"You tell me first," she insisted, unwilling to show any weakness to this man who'd had the power to love her forever or destroy her, yet had chosen the latter.

"Fine," he said abruptly. "When I asked Nagy to find me a wife, I had a clear picture in mind. I wanted a companion, someone to come home to at the end of the day who I can share my innermost thoughts with. Someone, most of all, who wants a child, or children. After you left me, I thought I could live my life without a family of my own, but as I grow older I find I can't see a future without a wife and children in it, nor do I want to be alone for the balance of my days. I guess it's part of the human condition to want

to be a part of something, to know a part of you will continue long after you're gone."

Imogene felt unexpected tears prick at her eyes. The words he'd chosen, his reasons for being here today, they were so similar to her own. How could they have this in common and yet be so wrong for each other at the same time?

Valentin continued, "Is that why you approached Nagy's company, too?"

"If I'd known it was your grandmother's company, I would have run in the other direction as fast as I could," she said defiantly. But then she softened, the fight spilling out of her. "Yes," she said simply. "That's exactly why I signed my contract. I want children in my life. Not just other people's children. My own. To love. Unconditionally. But more than that, I want a partner. Someone I can rely on. Someone I can trust."

Trust.

The word hung on the air between them. Valentin drew in a deep breath. Trust had been in short supply back in Africa, and not just within his marriage. All around them had been the constant threat of danger as a struggling government fought against corruption on every level. Even within the hospital there had been those he knew he could not rely on.

"Trust is a two-way street, is it not?" he asked gently.

"Always. You never had any reason not to trust me, Valentin. Ever."

"Whereas you feel you cannot trust me. That's what you're saying?"

"Based on past experience, what else can I say? You broke our marriage vows, not I."

The old frustration and anger bubbled from deep inside. She wouldn't listen to him back then; he doubted she'd listen to him now.

"So that leaves us at a stalemate, doesn't it? Unless you're prepared to put the past aside."

Imogene looked at him incredulously. "You think I should just forget you screwed another woman in our bed?" She deliberately chose strong language, not prepared to soften what he'd done by describing it with any moniker associated with the word *love*. "Just *put it aside* as if it didn't matter?"

"It doesn't matter because it never happened. Did you see me that day, Imogene? No, because I wasn't there. You wouldn't give me a chance to talk to you before having that lawyer serve papers on me. Perhaps you will at least do me that courtesy now." He pressed on, knowing he had a captive audience. It had bothered him intensely that Imogene never allowed him the opportunity to present his side of what she thought she'd seen. If anything it had underscored how wrong they'd been for each other that she'd been prepared to cast him in the villain's role so immediately. "Look, I know you were shocked to discover Carla in our house, let alone our bed. When

I gave her the key to the place it was supposed to be so she could get some sleep between shifts because the doctors' lounge had been appropriated for more patient beds. You know the crazy hours we were working and the volume of patients we had to deal with. Carla was overdue a break and I said she could use our place because it was close to the hospital. I didn't know she planned to have company. Imogene, I barely got to see you. If I had free time, why would I have spent it with her?"

"Why indeed," Imogene answered with an arch of her brow and a lift of her chin.

He let go a huff of irritation. "I wasn't the one with her that day."

"That's not what she led me to believe."

"She told you I was there?"

Imogene hesitated. Replayed the words in her head as she'd done so very many times before.

"Not in so many words," Imogene conceded.

"And yet you still don't believe me."

"I don't. I can't."

Hearing the underlying pain in her words made Valentin think again. She sounded as though she were in an internal battle. That maybe, just maybe, she wanted to believe him. He wondered how he'd feel in the same situation. Torn. Confused. And facing the realization that if she believed him, then that would have made the past seven years of loneliness and sorrow, the end of their marriage, all her fault. But it wasn't. While he had never been unfaithful to

Imogene, he knew he should have done more at the time to fight for their marriage—followed after her, insisted she see him instead of letting her hide in the only decent hotel in town until she flew out.

He knew Carla could be intimidating. The woman had a confidence many women he'd met lacked. She'd set her sights on Valentin as soon as he'd arrived on his volunteer service and they'd had a brief, intense fling. It wasn't until Imogene came on the scene that Carla had begun to eye him again, and she'd made it clear to everyone, Imogene included, that he was hers for the taking. But Carla had been wrong. From the minute Valentin had seen Imogene there had been only one woman for him.

She still was that woman.

Admitting that didn't come easily. Pride had always been an issue for him. A child prodigy, he wasn't used to making mistakes. His world had been filled with successes, each more glowing than the last. His failed marriage to Imogene had been the one black mark on the pristine blotter of his life. It was something he felt bound to rectify. If he could persuade her to give him, *them*, another chance, then maybe they could make things work.

His grandmother's words repeated in the back of his mind. *Be certain that you won't spend the rest of your lives wondering if you should have given each other another chance.* Would he regret it if he didn't try again? Looking at Imogene now, resplendent in her bridal gown—the same woman who'd

stood with him in a hurried civil ceremony all that time ago, and yet different in subtle ways he ached to explore—he knew the answer to that was a solid, unequivocal yes.

He chose his next words carefully. "So is there nothing I can do to persuade you to consider marrying me again?"

"I can't believe you even want to think about us marrying again," she shot back.

"Why not? Let's remove emotion from the equation and try to look at this logically. We both approached marriage this time in a more clinical fashion, and yet look at us. Here together again. Let's not discount the science that went into our pairing."

"Science!" She snorted in disbelief. "More like your grandmother's tampering with the results."

"And why would she do that if it would only make us unhappy?"

He knew he had made his point when she conceded.

"So what are you suggesting? That we give this a go? I'll be honest with you, Valentin. I don't hold hopes for things being any different than they were the first time. We may have gotten along in bed, but we had very little in common outside of it. Carla aside, and as difficult as it is to admit, I don't think we'd have lasted the distance. We met in a hothouse of extreme circumstances. It wasn't a normal relationship in any sense of the word."

"Then why not give it a chance and see how we do

in a more traditional setting? We're unlikely to find
another match that can make us both feel like this,"
he said, before reaching out one finger and tracing
the line of her lower lip.

Shock and desire warred with each other as he felt
her softness. Her warmth. The gasp of heated breath
as her lips parted. Every muscle in his body clenched
in anticipation of closing the distance between them.
Of tasting that tender flesh and discovering if she was
still as sweet, and as tart, as she used to be. Valentin
watched as a light flush colored Imogene's cheeks
and as her pupils dilated to almost consume her irises.

While she battled with her emotions, Valentin
pressed on. "Imogene, look at it this way. We have a
rock-solid prenup in force. We have a three-month out
clause. What have we got to lose?"

He saw her internal battle reflected in her eyes.
Heard it in her every ragged breath. Sensed the moment of weakness, the chink in her armor, and took
the opportunity to drive straight through it.

"And children, Imogene. Think about the kids we
would have together if it all worked out. The family we always wanted. I promise you, if you agree to
marry me again, you won't regret it. I will be faithful
to you. I will see to it that I meet your every need as
your husband and your life partner. I failed you last
time. I never fought for you the way I should have,
so I'm fighting for you now. I realize that I had tun-
nel vision when it came to my work, which left very
little beyond the physical for you. I never saw the

cracks when they appeared in our marriage. Never saw how vulnerable you had become. If I had been a better husband, you would never have jumped to the conclusion that I had been unfaithful. I won't let that happen again if you give us another chance. What will your answer be? Will you marry me?"

Three

She said yes.

Alice Horvath couldn't even begin to describe the sense of relief that overtook her when Valentin came out of the office and informed her the wedding would go ahead. She hadn't wanted to believe it wouldn't—she did, after all, trust her instincts wholeheartedly—and persuading others she was never wrong was rarely the issue, but it seemed that when it came to her grandsons, she was two for two, so far, on having her judgment questioned.

Valentin had gone to rejoin his brother, Galen, and a handful of cousins, who had congregated at the front of the function room. Alice took a moment to find her medication in her handbag before resuming

her seat. This darned pain in her chest was becoming tiresome. She certainly didn't have time for it now. She fought the urge to rub at it. It never did anything anyway. Ah, there was her pillbox. She popped a tablet under her tongue just as Imogene came out of the office.

"Are you all right, Mrs. Horvath?" she asked.

"I'm fine, my dear. And let me say that I'm so glad you've decided to go ahead with the wedding."

"Let's just say your grandson can be very persuasive."

Alice looked at the younger woman carefully. It was easy to see why Valentin had been attracted to her in the first place. The dark auburn hair and delightful figure aside, Imogene O'Connor had a rare exquisite beauty that was very clearly underlined with a strong personality and bright intelligence. During her background checks, Alice had discovered that over the past seven years, Imogene had grown her early-childhood centers into a business that had just been franchised nationwide. She was a strong and independent young woman with a good head on her shoulders, but it was the emotional side of Imogene that intrigued Alice most. She knew Imogene had rarely dated after her return from Africa. Whether it was because she was too busy for a new relationship or that she simply wasn't emotionally ready, Alice was glad the other woman hadn't rushed headlong into someone and something else.

When Alice looked at Valentin, with his aloof and

slightly dark nature, together with the bright flame of light this woman epitomized, she knew Imogene was unquestionably the yin to his yang. The computer data and her specialists had backed up her instincts completely. She would never have taken a risk with either of these young people's happiness otherwise. Life was just too precious, as she was becoming all too well aware.

The tablet continued to dissolve under her tongue, and incrementally the angina that had become such a plague in recent months began to ease. Alice inhaled carefully, relieved to feel the last of the tightness disappear, and directed a smile at the beautiful bride in front of her.

"Shall we return to the ceremony?" she asked.

"Perhaps you could ask my mom to join me again," Imogene said in a voice that was just a little indecisive. "I'd feel better with her beside me."

"Certainly." Alice turned to leave, then hesitated and looked back to Imogene before reaching out to take her hand and squeeze it lightly. "You won't regret this, you know. It may not be an easy road back to loving each other the way you did before. In fact, I hope the two of you discover a different kind of love this time. Something stronger, something that will endure. That's my wish for you and Valentin."

"It remains to be seen."

"Yes, it does. And it will take hard work from both of you."

Imogene gave her a nod and Alice turned away.

These two were going to have an interesting time of it—of that she was certain.

Imogene went through the motions, repeating the words uttered by the celebrant standing before her and listening to Valentin do the same. The service was simple, without the personal touches that it might have had if they'd planned this day together. In many ways it was about as detached as their first wedding had been, although the celebrant today tried to invest the ceremony with a great deal more joy than the slightly bored local official who'd performed their ceremony back in Africa.

Africa. She had to stop thinking about that time and comparing it to now. It was another world ago.

Today was a new beginning. One she'd agreed to pursue. She still wasn't even certain how Valentin had persuaded her to go ahead with it. All she knew was that with that one touch of his fingertip to her lips, he'd reminded her of the incendiary attraction they'd shared. Just one fingertip and she'd made a decision that would affect her for the rest of her life. Her entire body had reacted, concentrated on that mere touch. No one else had ever had the ability to set her alight with the brush of a finger the way he did. Which was a good thing, she'd always told herself as she'd pointed her attentions into her career and into establishing, then expanding, her business. Dating had been, for lack of a better word, a bland experience once she'd decided to test the waters again. But

that very blandness was what had put her in search of a matchmaking service that would find her something better than bland. Had she been unconsciously searching for a relationship like what she had with Valentin all along? The idea was as terrifying as it was exhilarating.

And more important, now that she had agreed to go ahead, where would they go from here?

"You may now kiss your bride."

The celebrant's words penetrated her thoughts, dragging her back to the reality that was her wedding day. Her eyes flared wide as she caught Valentin's smile and she froze in place. His eyes locked with hers, a serious expression reflecting back at her as he lifted her left hand to his lips and placed a kiss on her wedding finger.

"This is the ring you deserved all along," he murmured before leaning closer.

She barely caught her breath before she felt the pressure of his lips against hers. Sensation bloomed through her like a starburst, radiating to the tips of her fingers and the soles of her feet, not to mention everywhere in between. She parted her lips in response, kissing him back instinctively. Her hand rested on his chest for a brief moment before sliding up to his neck. The texture of his slightly long hair against her fingers sent another jolt of awareness surging through her and she lifted slightly upward. Valentin's arm curled around her waist, holding her to him.

It had always been like this between them. This

intensity. This overwhelming need to be close. Closer still. As if the world began and ended with each other.

"Um, guys?" Valentin's brother, Galen, interrupted them. "Care to leave something for the honeymoon?"

The gathered crowd laughed at his words and Valentin slowly drew away, leaving Imogene feeling more than a little stunned by what had just happened between them. Seven years. Actually, to be precise, seven years, three months, two weeks and five days since she'd walked out of his life. And still she was as hopelessly overcome by him.

"Are you okay?" Valentin asked gently, his arm still around her waist and his blue eyes searching her face for any signs of distress.

"Well, aside from my lipstick, which is probably demolished right now, I'm fine," she said as coolly as she could manage given the rapid beat of her pulse and the tingling shocks that still lingered in parts of her body that hadn't tingled in far too long.

He gave her a smile, took her hand again, and together they turned to face the assembly.

"I give you Mr. and Mrs. Horvath!" the celebrant triumphantly declared before surreptitiously wiping at his brow with a handkerchief.

They were married. Imogene couldn't quite believe it. Her synapses were still somewhat fried by that kiss. But there was no mistaking the strong fingers that were wrapped around her own, nor the steady presence of the dark-suited man standing beside her.

Her mother rushed forward, her cheeks still wet with tears, to congratulate them both. But as she drew back again she fixed Valentin with a stern eye.

"Don't mess it up this time, young man. You're lucky to get a second chance with my girl. Look after her."

"I will," Valentin promised.

Imogene felt a sting of embarrassment at her mother's words, but the gentle pressure of Valentin's hand signaled he'd taken no offense. She knew her mother would never understand why she'd made her choice to go ahead today. But then again, maybe she would. After all, her own husband had conducted many, albeit discreet, affairs during their marriage. Which was another reason Imogene had felt so strongly about infidelity. She'd always wondered why her mother had agreed to settle for less than 100 percent from her husband. Why she'd allowed other women to fill his life, where she rightly belonged. But then again her mother accepted a lot of things in the pursuit of her ordered life. Heavily involved in charity work, she enjoyed the distinction of being married to a leading international human rights lawyer. Of being perceived as calm and unflappable and the perfect hostess at all times. Imogene had learned early in her life that she wanted far more than that when she married. And she'd thought she had it with Valentin when they'd fallen so instantly and passionately in love.

Could they achieve that together again? She

thought of the words Alice had spoken to her just before the ceremony, about it not being an easy road back to loving each other again. Could they even hope to love each other again? she wondered. When she'd agreed to go ahead with this, the only thing she'd locked her mind onto was her main goal in this entire venture. A child, or children, of her own to love. But to love her husband, too? She flickered a glance up at Valentin. She wasn't sure if she could trust herself to trust him again, let alone love him.

Her insides clenched at the idea of making a baby. He'd made it patently clear he wanted children, too. Would that be enough to be the glue that would hold them together?

He also told you he was never unfaithful to you, a snide voice whispered in the back of her mind. In fact, he'd been adamant on that point, promising she had nothing to fear on that score. She wished she could believe him. Her eyes had told her a different story seven years ago. But she couldn't think about that now. She'd made her choice. She'd agreed to marry him and agreed that once their three-month trial period was up, if they were still together, they'd start trying for their family. And until then, she could only wait and see.

Valentin fought his frustration. He was never good with crowds, and this crowd was too happy, too noisy and very much too in his face. He had to concede that everyone here was celebrating his wedding, but

it didn't mean he had to like it. Not when every cell in his body urged him to take Imogene by the hand again and whisk her to where the helicopter waited on the expansive lawn outside so they could head to SeaTac, and then in one of the Horvath private jets to Rarotonga for their honeymoon. He couldn't wait for that part, but even though that kiss to seal their marriage had been better than everything he'd remembered, he knew that this time he and Imogene needed to tread carefully if they were going to make their union work.

He had no intention of creating a family without a strong foundation based on love and genuine trust in each other, no matter how well they survived the initial three-month trial period of their marriage. He wouldn't do that to her, nor would he do that to any child they might have. Their future happiness hinged on one thing: rebuilding Imogene's trust in him as her life partner. He had to do whatever it took if this was going to work. But it couldn't all be one way. He needed to be certain she was working just as hard on their future as he was. That she wouldn't run out on him again.

Losing her the first time had been crippling. He'd coped the only way he knew how, by throwing himself into things he could control, to a degree anyway. He'd signed on for another volunteer contract and did longer clinics, more surgeries and, even under the growing threat of civil war, more visits out into the bush. Some might say he'd had a death wish, be-

cause the political climate in the nation had become wildly volatile—driving many volunteers out—but for Valentin it allowed him to focus on what needed to be done and to tuck away the pain of distrust and abandonment that Imogene had left in her wake.

He looked across the room, to where she circulated among her friends. God, she was beautiful. But physical beauty aside, he knew she had depths he had yet to discover. Depths they'd never imagined of each other the first time around. And now they had another opportunity. When he'd seen her today he'd been shocked, but instinct had taken over. And while logic had protested, his body had rejoiced.

All of which brought him back to his thoughts of only a moment ago. He couldn't give in to that powerful pull they had between them. If he kissed her again, the way he truly wanted to, there was no way he'd be capable of pulling away.

Imogene's face lit up on a burst of laughter as one of her friends said something amusing. Again he felt the knot deep in his gut. He was going to have to do some serious workouts to burn off the sexual energy that had taken his body hostage since seeing Imogene again, because they had to take things slowly this time—to truly begin to know and understand each other better before losing themselves in physical sensations.

"So, having second thoughts?"

Valentin turned to face his brother, Galen. "No, should I?"

"I have to say I was worried there for a while at the beginning. I'd have laid odds that today wasn't about to go ahead and that my staff would be eating cake for the rest of the week."

Galen was head of the Horvath chain of resorts and was based here in Washington. Valentin allowed himself a small smile.

"Well, I'm glad I didn't have to inflict that on them."

Galen looked at him. "Something's different. Are you okay?"

"Why?"

"I don't know exactly. You were looking forward to this marriage, I know that much. But I was certain that when Imogene came down the aisle you would put a stop to it. You both seemed so adamant about it not going ahead. What changed your mind? Don't tell me Nagy put a spell on you both," Galen finished with a laugh.

Valentin paused for a moment. With his brother, he'd always been honest. With his cousin Ilya, too. The three men had grown up close. But for some reason he didn't want to put into actual words what had come over him when he'd made the decision to try to persuade Imogene to go ahead with the wedding.

"Maybe she did." It was all he would concede. "But it's early days yet. We have our three-month trial period to get through."

"You say that as if you don't believe it'll be easy."

"Nothing worthwhile ever is. We both know that,

right? And Imogene and I have a lot of work to do. Deep down she still believes I was unfaithful to her."

Galen spluttered his disbelief. "As if. You are the most loyal man I've ever known. So, who does she think you had an affair with?"

"One of the doctors I worked with."

"Was she hot?"

"Oh, yes, she's hot."

Galen stiffened beside him. "As in present-tense hot?"

He could always rely on his brother to be quick to pick up an unspoken thread. "Yes. As in she works for me now as head of research and development in New York."

Galen let out a slow whistle. "That could prove to be an issue. Have you told Imogene yet?"

"No, and I'm hoping we can overcome that before it becomes a problem."

"Well, if anyone can, you can, my brother. You deserve to be happy. I just hope that Imogene is the one you can find that happiness with."

"As do I. As do I."

Four

The jet was impressive; it even had its own master suite complete with luxury bathroom. Imogene wondered about the wisdom of having a bubble bath at thirty-six thousand feet but then pushed the idea aside. Right now, weariness dragged at every cell in her body and her mind. All she wanted to do was rest. She looked at the wide bed in the master bedroom and the expanse of fine Egyptian cotton that covered it. She knew it was fine because she'd touched it, her fingertips sliding over the silky softness of the high-thread-count fabric in absolute delight.

Valentin entered the room behind her.

"Tired?" he asked as he tugged his cravat loose from his throat.

"Shattered," she replied, feeling herself physically wilt.

It had been a tough day on so many levels, not least of which was discovering she was still powerfully attracted to her ex-husband. Well, new husband. She would never have believed he could talk her into agreeing to go ahead, but he'd been so convincing, almost making her believe that maybe she'd made a mistake all those years ago. That maybe she should have waited and listened before reacting. But then, given her own family situation, and her vehemence about never being in the same position as her mom, was it any surprise she'd reacted the way she had? Faced with the same situation, heaven forbid, wouldn't she do the same again?

She looked up at Valentin and saw the lines of strain on his face.

"You must be worn-out, too. I remember you never were one for grand social occasions."

"You remember correctly. Look, we have just over fourteen hours before we get to Rarotonga. We should get some sleep. Try to be fresh when we arrive at the Cook Islands."

"Did you want to take the bed?" she offered. "I can sleep in the main cabin."

"No, you take the bed. While you remember my discomfort with large social gatherings, I remember how you need to be comfortable to sleep."

Imogene felt her cheeks color at his words and the images that rapidly filled her mind. Of the two

of them in a narrow double bed doing anything but sleeping. Or when they did, and despite the intense heat of equatorial Africa, they curled so close together it was hard to tell where one ended and the other began. She'd grown used to sleeping with him so quickly after they'd met, and it had taken her months before she'd stopped reaching for him in the dark after she'd returned to New York.

She averted her gaze before she suggested something stupid, like sleeping together again. After all, they were married and had a common goal of creating a family together. But even as she thought it, she knew she wasn't ready to take that step. Not yet anyway.

"Thank you," she finally managed. "Would you like to use the bathroom first?"

Valentin laughed.

"What's so funny?" she asked.

"Us. We sound so damned civilized."

She giggled. "Yes, we do. Surprising under the circumstances, when you think about it."

"Shows we're better people than we were before." His eyes grew dark and serious. "I meant what I said back in that office, Imogene. Even more than the vows we exchanged. You won't regret this."

Imogene swallowed against the lump in her throat and gave him a small nod. She was beyond words, but she wasn't beyond feeling, she discovered as he strode through to the well-appointed bathroom and closed the door behind him. After a few minutes

she heard the shower begin to run. She groaned at the knowledge that he was naked, that water now coursed in strong rivulets over his body. A body she'd once known perhaps even better than her own. She slumped onto the bed and kicked off her shoes before tugging at the invisible side zipper on her gown. She stood again and let the gown drop to the floor before stepping out of it and picking it up again to gently fold it and lay it on an easy chair.

As she did so, she caught a glimpse of herself in the mirror. Dressed in a white lace-covered bustier and matching panties, together with white lace garters and sheer white stockings, she looked the epitome of bridal innocence. She touched the top of her thighs where her skin was exposed and felt a shiver course through her. Looks were one thing, but the actuality was quite another. Her entire body was attuned to every sound she could make out from the bathroom and it responded to the visual effects that her mind so willingly supplied.

The water snapped off and the sound propelled her into action. She grabbed her carry-on case and yanked out the robe she'd packed in there earlier. Had it only been this morning? It felt like a lifetime ago. She shook out the robe and gasped when she saw a shower of rose petals fall from the folds. The only person who could have sabotaged her things was her mom—she was the one Imogene had wanted with her all morning. And despite the lack of romance in her own marriage and her trepidation about the way

Imogene had approached this one, Caroline had attempted to inject a little romance into her daughter's day.

The door to the bathroom opened.

"You okay? I thought I heard you make a noise," Valentin said, stepping through the doorway with a white towel wrapped around his hips.

All rational thought fled. The perfect lines of his body could have been carved by Michelangelo, except she knew that if she touched him he wouldn't feel like cold marble. No, his skin would be hot, pliable and highly responsive to her caress. Every feminine instinct in her body clamored to be reacquainted with him. Intimately.

"Are those rose petals?" he asked, snapping her out of the seductive trance that threatened to take over her weary mind.

He drew closer and Imogene quickly shoved her arms in the sleeves of the robe and dragged it closed at her waist.

"Don't rush on my account," Valentin teased, the gleam in his eyes showing his appreciation of her attire.

"I'm sorry, I'll clean them up. Mom must have—"

"Hey, don't panic. It's okay." He reached out a steadying hand to her and clasped her forearm before she could bend down. "Relax, okay? I think a few rose petals are only to be expected with a bride and groom aboard, don't you?"

Heat flared along her arm. Heat that tantalized

and teased her already overwrought senses. Imogene pressed her lips together before answering, "But we're not your typical bride and groom, are we?"

"We never were typical," he agreed.

His words sent another rush of color to her cheeks. She groaned inwardly. Why did she continually blush around him? No one else had ever had the capacity to wring that kind of reaction from her before. She gestured to his towel.

"Are you planning to sleep in that?"

"It might give our cabin crew a bit of a shock if I did. No, I have some pajamas in my case. When you go to the bathroom I'll change in here, if that's okay."

Ah, so they were back to being polite again. That suited her just fine. Right now she didn't know what to think or say or do. All she knew was that she needed to create a bit of space between herself and Valentin before she did something stupid, like press her lips to the small brown discs of his nipples, or lick off that tiny droplet of water that followed the indentation of his abdomen.

"I'll say good-night now, then," she said stiffly and gathered up her toilet bag.

"Good night, Imogene," Valentin replied.

His voice was gentle and deep and almost her undoing. It would take only a second to lift her face to his. To claim a good-night kiss. But if she did, she knew exactly where that would lead and she knew she definitely wasn't ready for the ramifications of what would follow. Not mentally. Not yet.

* * *

Valentin looked out the aircraft window at the glorious coastline that appeared beneath them. Turquoise waters edged by foaming waves crashed against a reef that appeared to encircle the island they were approaching. As the plane drew lower still, he could make out white-sand beaches and towering palm trees that waved their fronds in the onshore breeze.

"Look at that," he said to Imogene, gesturing outside.

"It's beautiful," she answered, leaning across him to get a better look. "And it's certainly not like the New York winter we've left behind. Still, I guess, being in the southern hemisphere, it's summer down here, right?"

He grunted in response, barely able to speak right now. Did she know her breast was pressed against his arm, he wondered, or realize what her closeness was doing to him? How her subtle fragrance invaded his mind and made him think all kinds of inappropriate things he'd rather be doing with her right now? Her very nearness was going to be a major test of his ability to practice abstinence while they worked toward understanding each other better. It was something they were going to need to discuss very soon or he'd go crazy.

He moved slightly and Imogene immediately pulled away.

"Sorry," she murmured.

She fiddled with her seat belt, tugging at the strap and ensuring it was firmly done up.

"No problem," he responded, even though her touch had rapidly become a problem for him, indeed. He gestured out the window again. "Looks like we're coming in to land."

Imogene reached for his hand. "Do you mind? I always get nervous."

He curled his fingers around hers and was surprised at how tight her grip became as they descended through the clouds. "I never knew that about you."

"Well, we've never flown together before, so I guess you never got the chance to find out."

Her words came out lightly but he knew there was a lot more behind them.

"You're right," he conceded. "We didn't get to know a lot about each other at all, did we?"

The wheels touched the tarmac and her grip tightened even more. The plane felt like it was fighting the brakes as they eventually began to slow down and taxied toward the terminal building. One of the cabin crew came toward them, a warm smile wreathing her pretty face.

"We'll be disembarking soon," she informed them. "Once the stairs are down I'll come and get you and direct you to customs and immigration. It should only be a few minutes."

"Thanks, Jenny," Valentin acknowledged.

He felt Imogene disengage her fingers from his hand one by one.

"She's attractive, isn't she?" Imogene commented. "Do you know her well?"

Valentin shrugged, suddenly aware that any comment right now could be a potential minefield. "As well as I know any of the Horvath Aviation crews. I fly a lot with my work and I've gotten to know a few of them. Jenny's husband, Ash, is one of our pilots. It's company policy that if staff are a couple, they be assigned together whenever practical."

He felt Imogene relax a little. Was it because she now knew that Jenny was married? Until that supposed incident with Carla, jealousy had never been an issue, but was it going to be an issue now? Obviously Imogene felt vulnerable—she'd taken a major leap of faith in marrying him again, but then again so had he.

As soon as they were settled into their accommodations they'd be having a serious discussion about the boundaries of this new marriage of theirs and what they each expected out of it. Failure wasn't something that Valentin accepted, which was what had made him an excellent student, a brilliant doctor and an astute businessman. The fact that his first marriage had failed had always been a thorn in his side. He knew he'd been the innocent party all along but his failure in not being able to make Imogene see that had been hard to bear. Her insecurity had driven her away from him, which, in turn, meant he'd failed her. Now it was up to him to make sure she never felt that way again.

Before long they were descending the stairs of the aircraft and stepping onto the steaming-hot tarmac at the airport. It was a short walk to the small terminal building, and clearing customs and immigration took only a few minutes since they'd landed at a quiet time at the airport with no commercial airliners arriving or departing. The air around them was thick with humidity but a steady breeze blew off the nearby ocean and tugged at their clothing as they exited the terminal building to find a driver waiting for them with a sign.

"Kia orana!" the woman said in greeting as she slipped a lei of fragrant blooms around each of their necks. "Welcome to the Cook Islands. I'm Kimi and I'll be your contact and your driver during your stay with us. Please, come with me."

Valentin put a hand to Imogene's elbow as they followed Kimi to a van. Their luggage was loaded in the back and in a few moments they were off. After twenty minutes they were at their destination: a secluded villa just back from the sand on a private lagoon.

"Everything here is at your disposal," Kimi said expansively. "You have your own pool and you'll find water toys to use in the lagoon in the shed behind those bushes. There's an outdoor shower for you to use in complete privacy when you come back from the beach and if you need anything else here at the house, please just lift the phone over there and someone will handle

your query. I'm available to drive you anywhere you want to go.

"There's fruit and drinks in your kitchen, together with a few breakfast items, and you're welcome to use the neighboring resort restaurants for breakfast and lunch and just charge it back to the villa. Tonight, dinner will be brought to you at seven. We can serve it here on the patio or down on the sand if you'd prefer, although we're expecting a bit of a storm tonight. Oh, and there's a car or scooters for you to use if you want to drive around the island yourselves. Just remember to keep left and watch your speed. It's only thirty-two kilometers round-trip to get around the island, but you can take as long as you like. You're on island time now."

"Thank you, Kimi. This is lovely," Imogene said with a genuine smile.

He realized that beneath the smile, though, she still looked tightly drawn and tired. Obviously having that great big bed to herself during the flight hadn't ensured a good enough rest for her. Or maybe she was worried about something else. They'd essentially be alone here for the better part of seven days—was that what was bugging her?

Kimi bade them farewell and left.

"Well," said Imogene, with her hands on her hips and looking out to the tranquil lagoon. "Here we are. It's certainly beautiful."

"As are you," Valentin said softly. "You're going to need to be careful with that fair skin of yours."

"I brought plenty of sunblock," she said nervously as if she suddenly realized that he would be the one applying it in the areas she couldn't reach. "What time is it?"

"Just after 8:00 a.m.," he commented after glancing at his watch.

"Wow, it's going to feel like a long day, isn't it?"

"You can rest anytime you need. Our honeymoon is going to be all about doing what we want to do. And getting to know each other all over again. In fact, there's something we need to discuss."

She stiffened and drew away from him slightly. "Oh? And what's that?"

"Sex," he answered.

To his delight, color shot through her cheeks and her eyes flared in shock at his bluntness.

"S-sex?" she said on a wobbly note.

"I don't think we should do it."

Her eyes widened even farther. "You don't?"

He swallowed. This was all coming out wrong and even though it went against every male instinct in his body, it had to be said. "Obviously I want to… y'know. But last time we leaped into a sexual relationship so quickly it blurred everything else out of existence for us. We met, we married and we separated all within the space of only a few months. I think we should take our time this time. In fact, I'd like to…"

"You'd like to…?" she coaxed.

"I'd like to court you this time."

"Court me? Isn't that kind of like locking a stable door after the horse has bolted? We're already married."

"That doesn't mean we can't take the time now, this week at the very least, to get to know each other better." He took a step toward her and put his hands gently on her shoulders. "Imogene, this is important to me. I don't want anything to go wrong this time."

Five

Imogene looked at Valentin in surprise. There was a note to his voice she'd never heard before. He'd always been strong and decisive, and yet at this moment he sounded unsure. And for someone who was very much a take-charge kind of guy, he'd definitely put the ball in her court. Had he noticed how nervous she was? She'd never known him to be terribly observant of her before. His patients usually were the ones who got all of his focused attention and rightly so, but somewhere along the line, he'd changed. Either he'd expanded his powers of observation or he was truly making an effort for her. A warm kernel of hope lit deep inside. A hope that they'd be able to make this work this time around. She made her decision.

"Yes, I'd like you to court me," she replied with a shyness she hadn't expected to feel.

"Okay." Valentin exhaled on a long breath. "So, today—shall we go for a swim first, or would you like something to eat?"

"A swim sounds divine. We were fed so well on the flight I don't think I'm going to need to eat again for a while."

"Beach or pool?"

"Oh, beach, definitely."

Imogene walked off the patio and through the sliding doors into the house. Fans turned lazily on the ceiling, and she carried on walking until she found the master bedroom where their luggage had been put. There was another room on the other side of the hallway.

"I'll take this other room and leave you the master," she said, making a decision there and then.

To her relief, Valentin didn't protest. Instead he grabbed her cases and rolled them across the tiled floor to her bedroom.

"I'll knock on your door when I'm ready," he said with a grin. "It'll be like coming to pick you up on a date."

She smiled automatically in return. He really was taking this seriously. "Sure," she answered and closed the door behind him.

A flutter of nerves started low in her belly. It felt weird, yet exciting at the same time. Being courted by her husband? What a novel idea. She quickly opened

her case and lifted a filmy beach wrap out together with a bikini. She eyed the bikini with a little trepidation. Was this going to be too revealing? She hadn't worn one in such a long time she'd even felt uncomfortable trying it on in the store, but the sales assistant had been effusive in her compliments, saying the emerald green of the fabric worked brilliantly with her skin tone and brought out the color in her eyes. Well, Imogene decided as she began to shed her clothes, even if they were merely courting this week, no one said anything about not being tempting at the same time. In fact, wouldn't that just be normal?

A knock a few minutes later saw her tie the beach wrap firmly around her hips before opening the door.

"I'm ready," she said breathlessly. "I just need sunblock on my back, if that's okay."

"Yeah, sure," Valentin answered, taking the tube of lotion from her. "And if you can do the same for me, too?"

"Oh, yes," Imogene replied, hoping her fear at having to touch him, at having him touch her, wasn't clearly evident.

She was so attuned to his every movement, and while she'd agreed in principle to their no-sex agreement, actually living that agreement was going to be a challenge. But she, like Valentin, didn't want to muddy this chance at a new beginning by making the same mistakes they'd made before.

Mistakes? Had loving each other so absolutely been a total mistake? Unbidden, her body rode a wave

of remembered pleasure. She fought her scattered nerves back into submission. This was going to be a whole lot more challenging than she'd ever expected.

"Turn around," Valentin instructed.

She heard him squeeze a liberal dose of lotion into his hand, then felt the cold shock of it as he stroked it across her skin. The cold shock was rapidly replaced by the warmth of his palms as he firmly rubbed the lotion over her back and shoulders. When he got to the small of her back she drew in a sharp breath. That area had always been particularly sensitive for her and judging by the way his fingers lingered there, he remembered just what it did to her inside. After several taut minutes, he passed the tube over her shoulder.

"My turn," he said.

She swiveled around and took the tube from him, reluctantly meeting his gaze. There was an imp of mischief gleaming behind his blue eyes that tugged at her. He'd never shown a playful side of himself before. Everything about their last relationship, from their dangerous location and the risks involved with that, to the seriousness of his work and their own massive emotional highs followed by the deepest low of her life, had been borne on a power of emotion that had been exhausting at times. There'd been no time, no chance in that very different world, for flirtatiousness or fun. Given the contrast in their circumstances now, she found herself beginning to look forward to the rest of this week and dreading it

a little at the same time. What if they failed again? What if this week simply proved the only thing they had in common was sex? That wasn't basis enough for marriage or a family. They'd already proved that.

Imogene gestured for Valentin to turn around, hoping he wouldn't see the turmoil that churned inside her. The moment he presented his back to her she went to work, squeezing lotion into her hands and then massaging it into his broad, strong back. Her palms tingled at the touch. It had been so long, too long, since she'd touched anyone else like this and that it should be him... Well, that just made the experience all the more acute. Even though she thought she'd pushed all those memories into a dark place in the back of her mind, never to be taken into the light again, she still remembered him so well. Every line of his body. The dips, the hollows. Where he liked to be touched. Where he was ticklish. It was too much.

She gave him a slap on the shoulder. "That's it. I think we're covered."

"Thanks," he said, his voice rough.

"You okay?" she asked.

"Just a little uncomfortable," he admitted. "Only to be expected."

He turned to face her and her eyes dropped immediately below his waist where evidence of his discomfort disturbed the line of his swim shorts.

"Oh, I see," Imogene said, feeling an answering surge of need swell through her body.

"It's okay, Imogene. Just because I said we shouldn't

have sex while we work this out doesn't mean I won't desire you. It also doesn't mean there's any pressure on either of us. Just think of it as a normal healthy response."

"Normal, huh?" She looked down again, then back up to his face. "If you say so."

For a moment he looked surprised, then his face split in a grin before a chuckle rose from deep inside. Imogene felt her lips pull into an answering smile before she slipped past him and out to the covered patio, where she grabbed a couple of towels and headed down toward the gleaming white sand. That laugh, and the pleasure of seeing the sheer joy on his face, reminded her starkly of all they had missed together, of all that they had never had. Her eyes blurring with unexpected tears, she dropped the towels and her wrap on a hammock conveniently strung between two tall palms and carried on to the water's edge.

It was just tiredness that was causing this stupid reaction, she told herself as she looked across the lagoon. Behind her, she heard Valentin's rapid approach. She didn't have time to think before strong arms lifted her in the air and his forward motion propelled them both into the sea. She squealed just before they went under, feeling a brief moment of panic before she realized the water was warm and clear and she could easily touch the sandy floor.

Pushing herself upward, she let the water course from her face as she eyed her laughing husband.

"You looked like you needed a bit of help getting

in," he said by way of explanation, but that mischief she'd spied earlier belied his so-called helpfulness.

"Thanks," she said wryly. "Sometimes I guess you just need to take a leap of faith, right?"

His eyes grew serious. "Yes," he answered. "Like we did yesterday. A leap of faith is exactly what we need, Imogene. Faith in each other."

With that, he turned away from her and struck out with strong strokes toward the reef. Imogene watched him swim. Powerful, purposeful. Pretty much how he'd always done everything in his life when she'd known him. He seemed to believe they'd be okay, but as she started a gentle breaststroke through the water, staying nearer to the shore, where she felt comfortable, she still wasn't convinced. The specter of their past still stood like an unresolved invisible wall between them. Until she could believe him, wholeheartedly, it would always remain.

For the rest of the day they swam, ate and napped. The threatened storm hadn't yet appeared, so when it was time for dinner they elected to eat down on the sand by candlelight with the night breeze blowing past them and sand at their bare feet. The scent of frangipani wafted down from the garden and the palm fronds whispered constantly on the wind.

"What would you like to do tomorrow?" Valentin asked as he topped up Imogene's glass of champagne.

"I wouldn't mind seeing around the island. You know, get our bearings. What about you?"

"Sounds fun. I'm happy doing whatever you want."

"Valentin, this isn't just about what I want."

There was a note to Imogene's voice that struck a warning—some of that he put down to the sheer exhaustion she had to be feeling in the aftermath of their wedding and the travel. And even though they'd had a pretty easy day so far, he, too, felt tired tonight. But for the rest, he recognized immediately that she didn't want to be pandered to. He chose his next words carefully.

"No, I understand that," he answered with a smile. "Don't think you're going to get everything your way."

He got the response he'd hoped for when she gave a small laugh.

"Well, that's good to know, I think."

After dinner they got out one of the island maps that was tucked in a visitor guide on the coffee table inside the house and pored over it. After some discussion, they chose a few places they wanted to stop during their circuit of the island and marked others to visit on another day. They both agreed a week was probably not long enough for them to see everything they wanted, but they'd hit the highlights and play the rest by ear. By the time Valentin saw her to her room, and to bed, they were both dragging their feet.

"Sleep well, Imogene," he said, leaning forward and placing a gentle kiss on her cheek.

"You, too."

He waited until she closed her bedroom door

behind her and turned to his own room. He stood in the center of the floor for a moment, his hands fisted at his sides, willing his body to release the sexual tension that had gripped him all day. Today had been an exercise in torment. Whether it had been applying sunblock to Imogene's back or simply watching her swim or snooze in a hammock, he'd wanted her with an ache that verged on desperation. No other woman had ever had this effect on him and, he was certain, no other woman would. He had to earn her wholehearted trust back. He'd been given this second chance to make it work and he'd better not screw it up.

Which brought him back to the conversation he'd had with Galen about Carla. He'd have to tell Imogene at some stage about the other woman being on his staff, but he didn't think his honeymoon was the right place or time. No, he'd wait until they were home and in a routine. When they were feeling more comfortable together again instead of walking on eggshells and rediscovering their way with each other.

Which in turn brought him back to the one thing that had remained constant between him and Imogene through the seven-year absence they'd had from each other. The one thing that had brought them together in an incendiary conflagration to begin with—the overpowering strength of their attraction. Was it any wonder their relationship had burned up the way it did? Emotions had been high, passion

for each other even higher. In some ways he'd resented that at inopportune moments in his workday, his thoughts would turn to Imogene, or what they'd done together the previous night. Their relationship had been a puzzle to him and his ordered mind from day one, but he'd been unable to resist the attraction despite every logical part of his mind urging him to take things slowly and to tread with care. It didn't matter which way he dressed it up or tried to ignore it, then or now. He wanted her on a level that even he, with all his education and experience in life to date, could not quantify or explain. The only thing he could do was accept it and roll with it. No matter how much discomfort it left him in.

The next morning they elected to use the scooter to get around the island. Despite the heat that already stuck their clothes to their bodies, Valentin couldn't help feeling scooters were a vastly underrated method of travel because having Imogene plastered to his back, with her arms tightly wrapped around his waist as they drove on the island roads, was something he decided he'd like to get used to. Even with the cloying humidity that hung in the air after a heavy morning shower, he relished the feeling of her body pressed firmly against his. He was equally glad the low speed limit on the island ensured their trip took longer than he'd expected.

After a short ride, they strolled around the main center and a large colorful market before stopping

for lunch at a restaurant overlooking the harbor. The place thronged with people from all over the world, judging by the accents and languages they heard on the air, but overlaying everything was a sense of relaxation and casualness that left them both unwinding by degrees.

"This is some place, isn't it?" Imogene said as she watched a bunch of kids playing in the water.

"It sure is. Are you enjoying yourself so far?"

"Yeah," she said after a minute. "I am. It's been good to relax and kick back. I guess I didn't realize how tense I was before the wedding. Things have been really busy at work. I decided to take a step back from the active management of my company and get back to my roots as a teacher, but it's meant a huge amount of work. More than I imagined, to be honest. And when we get home it'll ramp up again when I start interviewing for my replacement as CEO."

"I heard you'd remodeled your company to create a franchise-based operation."

He watched as her eyes brightened and her face became animated as she explained the reasons behind what she'd done and how she'd put the new structure in place. It only increased his admiration for her. He'd never really understood her on this level before, but now, hearing her talk about her work like this opened up another window on the woman he'd remarried.

"My mother can't understand why I'd want to go back to teaching. She sees it as less important than being in charge of a company."

"Education, especially early education, is vital. If we can't teach kids a love of learning from their early days, it makes life more challenging for everyone as they grow up."

"Exactly. It's why my centers focus on finding out the best way for individuals to learn. Not everyone responds to the same style. And that's something I've really missed since I've been out of the classroom. Plus, I want a better work-life balance. I don't want my kids being raised by strangers while I pursue the next dollar. That's not what's important to me."

He loved listening to her speak so animatedly and wanted to know more.

"And your family? Are they excited for you with the changes? They must be proud of all you've achieved."

"Oh, they don't care one way or the other. Dad's attention is pretty much solely on his work and Mom is very busy with her charity committees. My work is peripheral to their interests."

She said the words lightly but he could hear the pain that lay beneath them. Valentin sensed the disconnect in her family was far wider than she'd let on. Her father hadn't even been there for their wedding, and while her mother had made the effort to be supportive, Caroline O'Connor had clearly thought the whole concept of marrying at first sight to be a ridiculous way to approach a marriage. She certainly hadn't looked any happier when she'd realized her daughter wasn't marrying a stranger after all, and

had remained coolly civil when conversing with him at the reception.

"You're not close?" he probed.

"I'm closer to my mom, but not to my dad. Oh, don't get me wrong, I'm sure he loves me in his way, but he's never been a hands-on parent. That's something I am determined to be and it's one of the reasons I restructured my company. I want to be there for my kids. For everything."

"We agree one hundred percent on that," he said, reaching across the table to take her hand.

The idea of them starting a family together filled him with a hope and excitement he hadn't expected.

"Good to know," she answered, tugging her hand free after a moment. "You lost your dad a while back. Do you have many memories of him?"

"I do, and good ones. He made an effort to be there for Galen and me. I get the impression that Mom was the rule maker on that issue because his work could easily have consumed him. Either way, until his heart attack he was a constant in our lives, even if he did struggle a bit with my incessant need to learn and understand the why of everything."

She laughed. "I've had kids like that from time to time. They're a challenge, all right. But they push you to be a better teacher in the long run."

Valentin looked across the table at her and smiled again. "Your classroom kids will be very lucky to have you back teaching."

"Thank you," she said. "That's one of the nicest things you've ever said to me."

He felt a jolt of shock. "Is it? Then it's something I definitely need to work on. You've a special talent, Imogene. I'm glad you're chasing your dream."

She looked a little flustered by his compliment and swiftly turned the attention back on him. "And you? Is Horvath Pharmaceuticals your dream or do you miss practicing medicine?"

"Yes and no. Working as a trauma surgeon was rewarding most of the time but there was always a disconnect between me and the people I treated. While I was saving lives, I was only the first port of call in what was often a long journey for them. It didn't bother me so much at first but as I've grown older I guess I've been looking for something different, something *more*, in my life. And when I looked at the work I was doing in Africa and the things that so often prevented us from making a lasting difference, I began to see where I might make a significant contribution. We were always hamstrung by a lack of supplies and medications to treat even the simplest of issues. Things that we take for granted that we can and will be treated for here. I went there to make a difference but what I did barely scratched the surface.

"When I returned home it only felt natural to go into the company business and work to try to make those vital medications more accessible for others. Not just overseas but at home, as well. The red tape can be suffocating at times but I like to remind myself

that I'm making a difference in improving people's lives and life expectancies."

The waiter chose that moment to bring their orders to the table, interrupting him. As soon as the guy had left Valentin felt as though the closeness that he and Imogene had begun to share had changed. Had it been his mention of Africa? Probably. He gave himself a mental kick and slowly turned their conversation to more general matters, exhorting himself to be more careful in the future. This relationship of theirs was a fragile thing and needed careful tending.

And the more time he spent with Imogene, the more he knew just how much he wanted their marriage to succeed. The thing was, did she? Was she as invested in trying to make this work and going past their three-month trial period, or was she simply marking off the days on the calendar? She wasn't as easy to read as she used to be and the realization troubled him more than he wanted to admit.

Six

Imogene lay in her tangled sheets fighting to get to sleep. The past six days had been incredible. Fun, even. It wasn't what she'd been expecting. Oh, sure, the physical attraction they'd always shared had simmered between them constantly. Even flared up a time or two in a way that had made her wish that one of them, at least, would do something to relieve it. Should she be the one to take the initiative? she wondered as she flopped onto her back and stared at the ceiling.

Of course not, she told herself. They had an agreement. They'd get to know each other better before taking that step. But then why did her body continually ache for his touch? Why did she wish he'd take her hand as they strolled along the beach, that

he'd kiss her as the sun set so gloriously, painting the sky with shades of purple and apricot and blush pink until the dark velvet of night consumed it all? Aside from those times when he helped her with her sunblock, he barely touched her at all.

She rolled onto her side and sighed heavily. Even though they were trying to get to know each other, they only hovered on the surface. It was as if they were each so determined not to cross any lines that they were almost being too careful, too respectful of each other's space. She sat up with a growl of frustration and pushed her sheets off. Maybe a nice cool swim in their pool would help, she decided.

She reached for a bikini, then looked at the glowing face of the digital clock at her bedside. It was 2:00 a.m. She was hardly likely to be observed by anybody else at this time of night, and with her nerves stretched to breaking point the idea of the silky soft glide of the pool water against her naked skin sounded like just the balm she needed.

Imogene grabbed her beach wrap and tied it around her before letting herself out of her room and padding on bare feet over the tiled floor. The humidity was higher than usual tonight; the air felt thick and cloying against her skin, making her scalp prickle and her hair cling to her face. The pool was looking better and better.

Outside, she heard the patter of a gentle rain on the patio. The night sky was obscured by clouds. She unwrapped the sheet of fabric from her body and walked

toward the pool, gasping a little as the rain hit her over-heated skin. She stood there for a moment, lifting her face to the sky and simply letting the rain fall on her.

There was something elemental about the night, about standing here alone, naked. With nothing between her and the rest of the world. No secrets, no shadows.

She walked the rest of the distance to the pool and dived cleanly into the water, staying below the surface for as long as she could hold her breath. Eventually, she popped up and drew in some air. She felt fantastic. The water slid around her, caressing her skin and soothing her fractured nerves. Maybe she needed to do this every night. She struck out for the end of the pool, determined to do some laps and to wear herself out so she could sleep, but the sensation of the water against her body only served to heighten the tension that had kept her awake. Yes, it felt divine, but at the same time it teased and tantalized. In fact, right now she felt more aroused than she had lying in bed thinking about Valentin.

She pushed herself harder, completing the laps more quickly, and once her muscles began to burn she slowed down again. Each lap got slower until she flipped onto her back and simply floated there on the surface while her heart rate and her breathing returned to normal. A gap in the clouds above revealed the twinkle of stars, and for the first time in a long time, Imogene simply allowed herself to be present in the moment. To empty her mind and to listen to the

night sounds around her, to feel the occasional drop of rain from the last of the stubborn clouds hanging overhead and to enjoy the steady *shush* of the waves on the beach not far away.

That was when she heard the shuffle of bare feet on the patio beside her. She looked across. It could only be one person. Valentin.

"Couldn't sleep?" he asked, squatting down beside the pool for a moment before sitting on the edge and letting his legs dangle in the water.

"No," she said, letting her feet drop down so her nakedness was not quite so obvious. "You, either?"

"Must be our night for it," he said before lowering himself into the pool.

He dropped down until his head was covered and then bobbed back up again.

"I'll, um, I'll leave you to it, then," she said, striking for the edge farthest from him.

"Don't leave on my account," he said. "In fact, stay. Please?"

It was the *please* that was her undoing. Even though every ounce of inner caution urged her to create distance between them, to avoid any chance of accidentally exposing her nakedness, she stayed right where she was. She knew it was risky but right now a part of her discovered that risk was looking pretty darned appealing.

"Sure, but could we turn off the pool lights?"

"Turn off…" Valentin's voice trailed to a halt as

understanding dawned. "Ah," he said eventually. "I see. How about I even the stakes?"

Before she could answer she saw him reach for his swimming trunks and seconds later they flew through the air to land on the poolside with a wet slap. Excitement buzzed in her veins along with a fair serving of trepidation. She knew how this was going to end. It was like watching a train wreck that you knew you couldn't halt. And in their case they already knew what the outcome would be like. They'd already traveled that road together. The one where passion ruled every waking moment of their lives, leading inexorably to their destruction. But they were better than that now, she told herself. They'd spent almost an entire week together without so much more than a chaste good-night kiss. They'd slept apart—well, *sleep* being a relative term given how many nights she'd tossed and turned alone in her bed.

Was this to be a turning point for them?

"Meet me halfway," Valentin coaxed from his end of the pool.

"And then?" she asked, her voice suddenly husky as a surge of desire dragged through her body.

"And then we'll see what happens next."

She didn't bother answering. In fact, she doubted she could form a cohesive sentence right now. Her blood fizzed in her veins as she pushed away from the edge of the pool and floated across to the middle. Valentin was already there, waiting with an expression on his face that drew the breath from her body.

Even in the pool light she could see a flush of need on his cheeks, a glitter in his eyes that told her far more than words ever could. He wanted her as much as she wanted him.

Without another thought she slid straight into his arms, wrapped her legs around his waist and felt like she'd finally found home.

"I've missed you," Valentin said as he supported Imogene in the water.

"Let's not talk about it, not when we have so many better things to do," Imogene said breathlessly before pressing her lips to his in a kiss that silenced them both.

She wasn't subtle. There was a carnality in her kiss that quite simply took his breath away. She made her position abundantly clear by silencing him as she had, but even as his body erupted with heat, and lust threatened to cloud his mind, he knew he wanted more than a physical release. Yes, she'd come to him willingly, without any hesitation, but he found himself wanting more than that. They'd only just begun the journey to understanding each other better this week and he was no closer to knowing why she'd been so quick to believe he'd been the wrongdoer in their first marriage. Why she'd been so adamant about not listening to his side of the story.

But then the heat of her body wiped thought from his mind. What was he doing thinking so darn hard when he had this beautiful, willing woman in his

arms? A woman he'd once loved with a force that had frightened him so much that when she'd walked away he'd immured his emotions—throwing himself into his work with scant regard for his safety on several occasions. He'd never understood, until he'd been served with the divorce papers, that one human being could hurt another so deeply without actually causing a physical injury. It had been an eye-opening shock. One he hadn't wanted to repeat, ever. His logical, quantitative mind had rejected the pain, told himself it wasn't reasonable, but reason took a hike in the face of what he'd experienced.

Imogene's tongue swept across his lips and reason took a hike all over again. His body responded in kind and tightened on a new energy that focused solely on the sensations that coursed through him, on the rightness of having her here in his arms, skin to skin, mouth fused to mouth, her inner heat poised over that part of him that ached with need. He kissed her back with a fervor that spoke of the years of denial he'd gone through, of how much he'd missed her, of how much he wanted her right here and now.

She shifted her body and the tip of his penis brushed the heated core of her. He shuddered and groaned, tightening his hold on her. In response her nails dug into his shoulders and she pressed her body more firmly against his, the tight points of her nipples imprinting on his chest. Valentin let one hand drift down her back, farther to the curve of her buttocks and farther still until he lightly caressed her opening. She

moaned into his mouth and let her head drop back. Her long hair swirled around them in the water, the tendrils brushing against him and setting off small electric charges with each touch.

He lowered his mouth to the smooth, pale column of her neck, licked against the pulse that fluttered there, nipped at the hollow beneath her earlobe and felt a tremor run through her from tip to toe. As delightful as this was, it wasn't enough. He wanted access to all of her and he couldn't do that here. He propelled them across the pool to the edge where he lifted her from the water and took a moment to enjoy the sight of the water coursing off her body, relishing how it skimmed over her pert, high breasts and shimmered over the lean muscles of her stomach and thighs.

"Had enough already?" she teased from her superior vantage point.

"Never enough," he growled and nudged her knees apart.

He heard her sharply indrawn breath as she realized his intentions. But she didn't pull away. Valentin trailed his fingers softly along her inner thighs. She was trembling now as she anticipated his next move but he took his time, letting his fingers drift closer to their eventual goal before skimming back down toward her knees.

"You never used to be this mean to me," she protested, as he let his fingers drift past her center again.

"This isn't mean," he assured her and bent his head

to kiss her creamy skin and follow the path his fingers had just taken. "This is merely taking my time."

Her legs tensed beneath his touch. He nuzzled against her, drawing in the scent that was a combination of her and the saltwater pool. And then he was there at her center. She leaned back and braced her arms behind her, spreading her legs wider to give him access to her sweet spot. He'd always loved this with her. Loved the taste of her, the sounds she made when he made love to her body the way he was doing now. He let his tongue trace around the bud he knew was supersensitive, not quite touching it but edging closer with each sweep. Her whole body shook now and he looked up, seeing her gaze on him, watching his every move. Without breaking their eye contact he pressed his lips to her clitoris and applied pressure with his tongue and his lips until her body grew so tightly strung he thought she might shatter into a million pieces. And then she did. Her climax hit in huge waves that left her limp with satisfaction.

So much had changed between them in the past seven years but this, this one incredibly special thing, remained the same. Valentin hauled himself out of the water and bent to lift Imogene into his arms. Holding her close to his body, he strode through to the house and into his bedroom. He took Imogene into his en suite, turned on the multihead shower and held her upright as water coursed over their bodies.

"You expect me to stand on my own after that?"

she asked, with a light, teasing note to her voice that had been missing for much of the past week.

"You can always lean against the wall," he said, smiling as he lathered up his hands and began to stroke them over her body.

She did as he suggested, murmuring her approval as he smoothed his hands over her breasts. He loved how neatly they fitted against the palms of his hands, how her pale pink nipples darkened as they tightened into peaks that begged to be kissed and sucked and lightly bitten. She let out a moan of pleasure as he did exactly that. Her hands came to rest on his shoulders, clinging as if he was all that stood between her remaining upright and collapsing into a heap on the floor of the shower. He finished washing her body, then rinsed her thoroughly. When her hands released their grip on his shoulders and began to move over his chest, he felt a swell of pleasure pour through him. If it was even possible, his erection grew harder, more demanding, as she stepped closer to him. His rigid flesh was trapped between them. The heat of her body on his sensitive skin was a delight and a torment.

Imogene reached for the shower gel and poured it over his chest, her free hand working it into a lather that slid down his body, teasing him further. She put the gel back on the shelf and then focused her attention on caressing his body. Across his chest, over his abdomen, then back up again to his shoulders, his arms, his back. Then finally, finally, she reached for

his aching flesh. Her slender fingers curled around him, her thumb gently rubbing his sensitive tip. He dropped his head into the crook of her neck and shoulder, and groaned out loud as she increased the pressure of her fingers, stroking up and down. In the end he couldn't take it anymore. He wrapped his fingers around hers to stop her.

"Let's take this to the bedroom," he said unevenly.

He reached for a towel and roughly dried her before scraping it quickly across his body. Then he took Imogene by the hand and led her to the sheet-tossed bed he'd left not so long ago. He'd gone in search of surcease. Instead, he'd found his wife.

While Imogene lay down on the bed, he reached for the bedside table drawer and pulled out a condom. He sheathed himself and in seconds they lay on the bed together—hands reaching, legs tangling, mouths meshing until there was no clear delineation between where he ended and she began. He rolled her under his body. Her legs shifted to allow him to settle between them and then he was nudging at her entrance. The head of his penis bathed in the heat of her body. He surged forward, his rhythm uneven at first as he fought to stay in control. But then their synchronicity of old reasserted itself.

Valentin felt Imogene's body tighten around him, heard the keening cry that spilled from her lips as her second orgasm flooded her body. Then and only then did he let go. Pleasure shot through every inch

of his body and his mind. This perfection was what he'd been missing for far too long—this, and the incredible woman in his arms.

His woman.

Seven

Imogene sat next to Valentin in the Horvath jet as they flew back over the Pacific and away from their island paradise idyll. Waking in his bed this morning had felt all kinds of right and all kinds of wrong at the same time. Her entire body still hummed with the aftermath of his lovemaking. A part of her had wanted to start their day with a reenactment of their middle-of-the-night passion, but logic had dictated she slip from his bed and go to her room to shower and dress before their flight home.

They'd barely spoken. As if both of them were too lost in their thoughts about what they'd shared and where they should go next. Their physical compatibility was a given. He'd only had to touch her and she'd

gone up in flames and, she suspected, it was much the same for him, too. Beneath all of that, however, was a deep sense of disappointment in herself. They'd both allowed physical needs to overwhelm the agreement they'd made to take things slowly. Oh, sure, they'd waited—what—six days before acting on the simmering tension that hovered between them? That was hardly admirable. And while she knew she could argue with herself until she was blue in the face about the fact that they were adults with needs and were perfectly entitled to have incredibly amazing sex if they wanted to, deep down she knew it was wrong.

There was still so much unresolved between them. So much left unsaid. And while they had no trouble communicating with their bodies, their ability to open up to each other verbally continued to be an issue. In this entire week together, they'd stuck to peripheral topics, barely skimming the surface of who they really were or what they each truly wanted—out of their remarriage or out of life in general. And she was mad at herself. This week had been her opportunity to reach out and discover if Valentin really had changed from the man she'd left back in Africa. Whether she honestly could trust him again. All she'd discovered was that she couldn't trust herself around him. Hormones, it seemed, ruled over her head whenever she was around him.

Even now, seated next to him on the plane. The seats were large enough that they weren't even touching and yet she could feel the imprint of his

body next to her as if they were. The heat of him, his scent, the sound of his steady breathing. Every little thing about him. She shifted in her seat and looked out the window beside her. Nothing but clouds. A bit like how her brain felt right now. She sighed.

"Everything okay?" Valentin asked, leaning closer.

A gentle waft of his cologne invaded her senses and sent a shaft of longing through her body. She clenched her inner muscles on an involuntary wave of need and fought the urge to close the distance between them. To assure him with her lips and her hands that everything was just peachy.

"I'm fine," she muttered through clenched teeth.

"Forgive me for saying this but you neither look nor sound fine."

She turned to face him and caught the twinkle of humor in his eyes. "It's not a laughing matter," she said sharply.

His humor dimmed immediately. "No, you're right, it's not. But it's done. We went against our own edicts. I hope you're not going to sulk about that all the way home."

"Sulk? You think this is sulking?" Outrage fired every nerve in her body. "I'm angry, if you must know."

"Thank you for communicating that," he answered calmly.

His calm only served to fuel her irritation. "Angry at you," she spit.

"I accept that."

She rode the wave of tension in her body for a split second longer before it ran out of her in a rush of helplessness. Sagging into her seat, she added, "And angry at myself."

"And that's the problem, isn't it?"

"Yes. What are we going to do, Valentin?"

He sighed. "Exercise more restraint in the future, I imagine. I'm equally annoyed with myself, but you can't say it wasn't a memorable experience. In fact, given the same opportunity, I would do it all again. Do you have any idea how alluring you looked swimming in the water naked?" His voice dropped, grew deeper, thicker. "Your hair spread out around you. The pool lights illuminating your ivory skin. You were otherworldly. A water nymph set to ensnare me. I was in your thrall. Seeing you like that brought back every memory of our life together before. Every kiss, every caress—every time we made love until we could barely breathe anymore. And I wanted you. I'm not ashamed of that. I still want you, Imogene."

Imogene felt her eyes fill with tears at the depth of emotion in Valentin's voice. He'd never spoken to her like this before. Never been this honest about his feelings for her.

"But we both know where wanting will lead," he continued. "And it's not enough, is it?"

Sorrow pierced her heart. "No, it wasn't before… It isn't now."

"We have more work to do before we allow ourselves the pleasure of each other again. Agreed?"

She nodded solemnly. "Agreed."

Even though she knew he was right, it didn't prevent regret from filling every empty space inside. She'd missed the physical side of a relationship, and the physical side of anything to do with Valentin had always been the pinnacle of perfection. It was just everything else that had destroyed her. That was what she had to remember. That was what she had to work on.

"Imogene?" he prompted when she fell silent again.

"Hmm?"

"We can do this. I want to understand you better. I want you to understand me. And I want the physical aspect of our marriage, too. I'm prepared to wait so we can get the rest right this time."

"Thank you," she said softly in response. "It means a lot to me."

"You mean a lot to me. You always did."

He'd hurt her so very badly. Had expected her to simply believe him when he said he hadn't slept with Carla since their marriage. Hadn't understood what she'd seen, what she'd been told, and had made no effort to. He'd made his statement, he'd stood by that and he'd expected her to believe him. But she couldn't believe him. Not when she'd seen what she'd seen. And not when he exhibited every last trait of her father's, a man made more attractive by his devotion to his duty, by his single-minded focus on what was

right. Add into the mix his physical attributes and the adoration of the people around him and you had a dangerous mix. She'd always sworn she'd never marry a man like her father. Not for her, the life her mom had chosen—being a token wife while he pursued his calling and dallied in multiple sycophantic relationships.

Was it too much to expect devotion from your partner? To be married to a man who saw fidelity as necessary in a successful marriage? No. Not in her book. And until she could be certain that Valentin was capable of that, she had to ensure she kept her guard very firmly up. Yes, she'd agreed to give this marriage a second chance, with the hope that one day she could have the children she dearly wanted. But she wasn't going to put her heart on the chopping block for Valentin Horvath to destroy again.

She had to be certain.

By the time they landed in New York they were both shattered. The layover time in Los Angeles had seemed to go on forever but at least they'd been able to sleep while in the air. Valentin thanked their driver after they pulled up outside his apartment building on Fifth Avenue. Light flurries swirled around them and across the road Central Park was shrouded in ice and snow. The wintry January climate was a vast change from the warm, humid air of Rarotonga.

"I'll take care of our cases, Anton. You head on

home to your wife and kids," he said as the man removed their cases from the trunk of the limousine.

"Not a problem, Mr. Horvath."

"Seriously. It's already past eight o'clock and I
know how much you love reading to your girls."

"Then thank you, sir. I'll pick you up at seven for
work?"

"Make it a little later tomorrow. Maybe eight?"

"Whatever you say," Anton said with a smile. "Enjoy
your night, sir. Ma'am."

Imogene gave Anton a distracted smile and reached
for the handle on her case as the car pulled away from
the curb.

"How could I forget how cold it is here?" she grumbled.

"It's not Rarotonga, that's for sure. Here, let me
take that," Valentin offered.

"Thanks," she replied and looked skyward at the
Neo-Italian Renaissance–style exterior of the build-
ing. "I had no idea you lived on the Upper East Side.
Have you been here long?"

"Since coming back from Africa. I love looking
over the park."

"I bet the view is stunning."

"It is, although we'll have to wait for a clear day
for you to fully appreciate it. Let's go up."

After a nod to the doorman and the concierge,
they traveled up in a mirrored and wood-lined elevator that looked as if it was original to the building

but ran as if it had been built yesterday. Smooth and silent. The doors slid open on the top floor.

"Penthouse, no less," she commented.

Valentin wondered if she was regretting subletting her brownstone apartment in Brooklyn about now. Or if she was wishing that they'd kept separate homes while they found their way back into a lasting relationship.

"I saw it and couldn't resist." He gestured, dragging their cases onto the parquet floor of the vestibule.

"Wait, this is it? We're here? No corridor, no separate entry?"

Valentin chuckled, the first time he'd felt any sense of humor for a while. He gestured back to the elevator. "This not enough of an entry point for you?"

"Oh, it is. I just…" She seemed at a loss for words as she peeked from the vestibule into the main foyer that led to his formal rooms. "This is huge. You have the whole floor?"

He shrugged. "Should I apologize for that?"

"N-n-no," she stammered. "I'm just a bit surprised, to be honest."

"Surprised?"

"You were such a minimalist back in Africa, and let's face it, this is hardly a bachelor pad." She looked to the rooms beyond the entranceway. "It's a real home."

"Is that a problem?"

"No, of course not, but it's very different from

what we had before. I don't know what I expected—
I just never pictured you in a setting like this." She
seemed flustered as she stepped through the foyer
and into his library, moving straight to the windows
that overlooked the park. "Wow, this is beautiful. It's
like stepping back into the thirties."

He followed close behind, leaving their cases in
the foyer. "Close. Mid-1920s, to be precise. I had the
choice to renovate extensively, or preserve the special
character of the apartment. It had been in the same
family for years before I bought it and it seemed a
shame to wipe all that history out and replace it with
something with less soul. Less heart."

She looked at him in surprise.

"What?" he asked. "You don't think I have a
heart?"

A tinge of pink touched her cheeks and she busied
herself undoing the buttons on her cashmere coat.
"No, it's not that. It's just that every now and then I
realize how much I don't know you."

He reached a hand out and touched her forearm.
"That's what this is about for us now, Imogene—
rediscovering each other. We can do this. Day by
day, okay?"

She put her hand over his and squeezed. It was
the first time she'd voluntarily touched him since last
night. Or was it the night before? They'd been traveling
so long he'd grown confused with all the time zones.

"I'll show you to your room, let you freshen up and then show you around the apartment, okay?"

"Sounds like a good idea," she said, letting him go.

He felt the loss instantly and wished he could simply take her hand, like a normal couple, and tug her down the hallway to *their* bedroom, not hers and not his. He closed his eyes briefly and took in a steadying breath. All in good time. Back in the foyer he snagged their cases and then led Imogene down the hallway toward the larger of the guest bedrooms.

"This is yours and you'll find the bathroom through there. It connects to the next room but there's no one in there. My room is farther down the hall and Dion's room is on the other side of the apartment."

"Dion?"

"My butler-slash-maid. But don't let him hear me call him that. He prefers the term *general factotum*." Valentin forced a smile. "He came with the property and takes his role very seriously. His family served the family who owned the apartment before I did. He's also a darn fine cook, so there was no way I was encouraging him to retire after he fed me the first week after I moved in."

"Where is he now?"

"I sent him to visit his daughter while we were on honeymoon. She lives in Vermont. He'll be back tomorrow."

"And his wife?"

"He's a widower." Valentin put her case on one

side of the room. "When you're ready, come down the hall to the master bedroom to get me and I'll take you on a tour."

"Okay, I'll do that."

Valentin turned to go but hesitated at the door for a moment before turning back to face her again. "We're going to make it this time," he said with more force than he intended.

Imogene locked gazes with him and they stood there like that for several seconds. She was about to say something when his mobile phone chimed. He slid it from his pocket and looked at the display.

"It's Galen. I probably ought to take this."

"Please, go ahead."

He went down the hall, answering as he entered his bedroom.

"Galen, good timing. We just got back."

But it was his brother's next words that drove him to his knees. "Nick and Sarah, they're dead."

Galen's college buddy and his wife had been instrumental in helping Galen build the Port Ludlow resort into the successful business it was today. They were his best friends and, together with their nine-year-old daughter, Ellie, had spent a lot of time with the Horvath family over the years. So much so, they were like honorary members of the extended clan. But dead?

Valentin listened as Galen outlined the details of the accident that had taken his best friends' lives. Felt his brother's grief in every syllable.

"And Ellie?" He was almost too afraid to ask.

"She's devastated, poor kid. I've got her staying with me. Her class was on a school trip, thank God, otherwise she might have—" Galen's voice broke off.

Valentin filled the gap instantly. "What's going to happen to her? They didn't have much in the way of family, did they?"

"No," his brother answered brokenly. "Just us, really. Nick asked me years ago if I'd agree to be Ellie's guardian if something like this happened and of course I said yes. I just never thought…"

"You're not alone, Galen. And neither is Ellie. We'll all help where we can. In fact, I'll come tomorrow," Valentin offered.

"No, don't do that. You're just back from your honeymoon. I wouldn't ask it of you even if you weren't. There's nothing anyone can do."

"The funeral, then. We'll both come."

"Thank you, I'd appreciate it. So would Ellie. You know how much she adores you."

"As I do her," Valentin said grimly. The poor kid. Alone now. No, he told himself. Not alone. She had Galen and she had the rest of his family to buoy her through this awful time. "I'll call you again tomorrow, okay?"

"Yeah, thanks. I should have more details then. In the morning I have meetings with the lawyers regarding guardianship and Nick's and Sarah's effects."

"It's not going to be easy, but you'll get through

it. They're counting on you now. Remember I'm here if you need me. For anything, okay?"

He hung up the phone and sat with his back against his bed. The news was sobering, proof that life could change in a split second.

"Valentin? Bad news?"

He looked up to see Imogene hovering in the doorway. He gestured for her to come in and explained what had happened. Instantly compassion flooded her features.

"That poor girl. Poor Galen. Is he going to be okay?"

"I guess, but he certainly didn't ever count on becoming an instant parent."

"Kind of makes our problems dim in comparison, doesn't it?" she said with an empathy he heartily appreciated.

"It certainly does. We'll go for the funeral. I'll let you know when I have the details."

"Of course," she said. "Look, you've had a shock, can I get you something? Make you some hot chocolate, maybe?"

He looked up at her and nodded. "Yeah, I'd like that."

"Then you better show me where the kitchen is," she said with a gentle smile.

She held out her hand and he grasped it firmly, allowing her to help him to his feet. And he made himself a silent promise. This would work between them, come what may. He didn't want a life of regret—to

look back and wish he'd done things differently or better. Through their match made in marriage his grandmother had given them a second chance at love. It was up to him to ensure it didn't get messed up.

Eight

It was hard to believe they'd been married a month already. That week in Rarotonga, that magical night—those memories had been shoved firmly in the past by a New York winter and both her and Valentin's getting back to work. But tonight, she wanted to mark the occasion and she'd asked Dion to help her create a delicious taste sensation as a special dinner. Dion had been only too happy to help.

If only it had been summer, she thought, even spring. Then they could have dined on the garden terrace upstairs. Of course it was covered with snow right now and still bitterly cold, so the dining room would have to do. Or maybe a picnic in front of the fireplace in the library—now, there was an idea. She

nibbled at her lip as she pondered the logistics. Beef Wellington served off a plate on the floor? Probably not the best plan.

Despite their agreement to get to know each other better, they'd both been shoved straight back into the demands of their jobs from the day they'd returned to work. Weekends had been busy, too. Their first weekend home they'd flown back to Seattle to attend the funeral of Galen's best friends. It had been a terribly sad experience, but the way Galen had supported Ellie, and the way all the Horvaths had shown their support for them both, had been balm for the soul.

There was no doubt Galen loved that little girl as if she were his own and he was doing everything in his power to assure her of that fact. It had been an eye-opener for Imogene, too, to see that Valentin was equally protective of the child. It had shown a new facet of his character that gave her some inkling as to what he'd be like as a father.

She flickered a glance at the calendar on the wall. Two more months until they'd have to make a decision about whether their marriage would go ahead. While she hadn't seen any evidence to support her fears that he shared her father's attitude to marriage, she still felt as though Valentin was holding something back. Sure, they'd spent the past few weeks sharing their evenings, debating politics, discussing aspects of their work, but she still sensed something was missing. She'd learned more about Valentin's childhood—a challenging one for all concerned, given his high intelligence and burn-

ing need to learn. Even now he spent a lot of his free time poring over textbooks or scientific essays, all in the pursuit of being better educated and well-informed so that nothing would surprise him in the course of his work. That need in him to know all fascinated and amused her. It seemed that to Valentin everything was quantifiable and, she supposed, in his world it probably was. A smile tugged at her lips as she considered how he'd cope in one of her day cares for a week. With varying age groups of children in various stages of willfulness. One thing was consistent in childcare and early education—no two days were ever the same.

Imogene sighed wistfully. She'd missed that. The color and noise of the classrooms. The bright eager minds as yet unformed by societal pressures or the idea that there was anything they should not or could not do. She looked forward to being back in that environment. Next month would see the appointment of her replacement as CEO. Only a few months ago that had been a topic under discussion and now it was happening. Change was constant. That was never truer, she realized as she considered her own position. So on that basis, it was logical to assume that *if* Valentin *had* cheated on her seven years ago, he was capable of change now. She had to learn to let go of that dark place in their past. To put it in a box in the back of her memory and fully embrace this fresh new start that they were both skirting every day.

The timer beeped on the oven, distracting her from the direction of her thoughts. She was just about

to check on the beef Wellington when her phone rang. She recognized the chime instantly. Valentin. She couldn't help the tiny flutter of excitement that struck when she answered and heard the timbre of his voice in her ear.

"Imogene? How are you?"

"Looking forward to seeing you," she said, deciding to take the bull by the horns and to stop denying the fact that hearing from her husband thrilled her. "I have something special planned for when you get home."

There was a long pause as he obviously digested her words, and Imogene felt her stomach drop by degrees.

"Oh, Genie," he sighed across the phone line, regret heavy in his voice. "I'm so sorry. Something has come up at work that requires all my attention right now. I won't be home until late. It's why I was calling."

She realized that for the first time since she'd walked out on him, he'd called her by the nickname only he had ever used. The sound of it falling so easily from his lips was a balm to her soul. A reminder that even though they were still treading so carefully with each other, there was emotion between them and a growing trust. She fought back her disappointment that he was working late and focused instead on him. He sounded tired, frustrated. And she wanted to resolve that for him—to take away the guilt that reverberated in every word.

"Don't worry, Valentin. I'll be here when you get home. We can do something special another time."

"I'm really sorry," he repeated. "If I could get out of it, I would. We're so close to closing this deal but there's been a hiccup in the development budget that requires urgent work."

"It's okay. I understand. Things happen. Please, don't worry."

"I feel bad. Since we've been back I've been working all hours. That wasn't my plan."

She had to admit that she felt a little as though they'd slid immediately back into their old roles. Him working all the hours while she waited at home for him. Except this time around she'd been busy, too. There'd been days when he'd beaten her home because she'd been interviewing candidates for the CEO role or tied up in other matters that couldn't be taken care of during business hours. She got it. When you were in charge the buck stopped with you and you had to deal with it. She could hardly complain when something came up that he hadn't anticipated.

"Valentin, please, don't worry. It can wait."

"I'll make it up to you, I promise."

"I'll look forward to that," she said, smiling.

They said their goodbyes and she turned to survey the kitchen and her preparations to make tonight special for them. Yes, she was disappointed but at least she'd matured enough now not to take that out on him. Not like she used to before. It was a sober-

ing realization and she was still lost in thought when Dion entered the kitchen.

"Was that Mr. Horvath?" he asked.

"Yes, it seems he has to work late tonight."

"That's a shame. Would you like me to finish up in here and put things away?"

Imogene thought for a moment, then shook her head. "No, I want you to help me find a way to take all this to him. If the mountain won't come home for dinner, then I'll just have to take dinner to the mountain."

Dion's wrinkled face creased into a smile. "That sounds like a perfect solution, madam. I have just the equipment you'll need. You go and get ready and leave the rest to me. I'll order the car to be out front for you in half an hour."

"Excellent, thank you, Dion. I appreciate your help."

"It's what I'm here for, madam," the older man said with a twinkle in his eyes.

Imogene fled for her bedroom. Suddenly tonight was looking a whole lot more interesting after all.

From the moment he'd ended his call with Imogene he hadn't been able to concentrate. The spreadsheets on his computer had begun to blur and all he could focus on was the hastily disguised disappointment that had been in her voice when he'd said he wasn't coming home for dinner. He looked at the date at the bottom of his computer screen and understand-

ing dawned. He was such an idiot. How could he have overlooked that today was a month since their wedding? And it augured well for their marriage that she'd wanted to mark the occasion. Not so great was the fact that he hadn't even noticed.

Guilt slashed across his mind. His obsession with work had been a major player in the discontent in their first marriage. His hours had led to more than one argument at home. Arguments that had ended with passionate lovemaking and promises to try harder but that hadn't saved his marriage in the end. Nor would they now if he didn't improve his awareness.

He was torn. Instinct told him to get up from his desk and head home to his waiting wife. Logic told him that one more pass of the spreadsheets would allow him to see exactly where the problem lay. It wasn't like Carla to make a mistake in her budgets, but the flaw in the calculations that he'd been provided with could derail this whole deal by ballooning the costs.

A sound at the door made him look up. As if he'd conjured her up with his imagination, there was his wife. She wore her cashmere coat buttoned up to the neck and a pair of sinfully high pumps that highlighted her slender ankles and finely muscled calves. Her hair was up in one of those twists that looked entirely feminine and exposed the delicious sweep of her slender neck. A pair of diamond studs glinted in her earlobes. Valentin felt a jolt of sexual aware-

ness, but as had become his habit since their return from their honeymoon, he quelled it just as quickly as it arose.

"Imogene?" he said, pushing up out of his chair and going to meet her. "This is a surprise."

"A good one, I hope," she said, holding the door open with her foot and maneuvering a small cart through the door from behind her.

A delicious scent permeated the air in his office and Valentin stood, rooted in shock. "You brought me dinner?"

"Happy monthiversary," she replied with a satisfied smile on her face. "Now, where would you like me to put this?"

When he was too stunned to reply she carried on as if his response wasn't necessary.

"Okay, how about over by the window? Dion assures me that this folds out into a little table, so maybe if you could bring a couple of chairs over…?"

She gestured to the two guest chairs sitting opposite his desk and he hastened to comply. While he did so, Imogene undid the buttons on her coat and shrugged it off her shoulders. Any and all attempts at controlling his libido were moot at that point as she revealed a figure-hugging dress that ended high above her knees. Long-sleeved, it gave the impression of demureness— the boat neckline skimming across her collarbones modestly and the rich purple fabric making her skin appear to glow. But when she turned around to fold out two sides on the cart and apply the brake, she exposed

her back—bare from nape to just below her waist with a drapey thing of fabric that hung like a shawl around the edges. His mouth dried and his hands clenched on the back of the chair he was carrying. The rest of his body? Well, that just went up in flames.

Imogene continued to set up her surprise for him, shaking a pristine white tablecloth over the makeshift table. Then she reached underneath the trolley, pulled out several dishes together with plates and cutlery and set it all on the table. She even had a small posy of flowers in a crystal bowl in the center. Throughout, she remained oblivious to the torment she was inadvertently putting him through. Or was it inadvertent? They'd been married a month. They'd been "dating" when time permitted. They'd observed all the rules they themselves had set in place. Was it too much to wish that they—no, *she*—was ready to take it up to the next level?

"I was going to bring candles, too," she said, straightening a knife beside one of the plates. "But I wasn't sure what the regulations were in your building regarding open flames."

He was speechless. She'd gone to all this trouble for him. No, he corrected himself again, for *them*. Which only served to make it all the more special. He carried the second chair over to the table and the moment his hands were free he reached for her, pulling her close.

"You are an incredible woman," he said. "Thank you."

"If there's anything I've learned in the past seven years, it's that if I want something, I have to reach for it myself. I can't just sit around waiting for things to happen or expect other people to do things for me."

He looked into her eyes, more green than gray tonight, and felt himself fall a whole lot in love with her all over again. This was it. The real thing. He had been an idiot to let her go before, and he wasn't going to let that happen ever again.

"Shall we eat?" Imogene said, interrupting his intention to show her exactly how he was feeling right now.

"Sure," he replied, releasing her and turning to the table. "You did all this yourself?"

"I had a little help from Dion but he mostly just supervised. Seems he's quite the romantic beneath that hoary exterior."

Valentin suspected it had a lot more to do with the nature of the beautiful woman in front of him and how she brought light into every place she went rather than Dion's romantic side. He held her chair out for her, bending over her slightly as she settled herself. Her scent wafted up to him. Fresh and clean and with that little something spicy underlying it— the spiciness a reminder of Imogene's hidden depths. His fingers tightened on the back of her chair as he pushed it in. If they were a normal couple he'd have kissed the exposed nape of her neck just now. But, he reminded himself, they weren't like other couples. Instead, they were a couple working their way back

to where they ought to be, from a past fraught with suspicion and misconceptions. They had both been immature about relationships that first time. Obeying the demands of their bodies over any semblance of rational thought. It was no wonder they'd crashed and burned. But this, tonight, it was a symbol of what they were building together. Something with strong bones, a joint purpose. Hope.

Before they ate, Valentin adjusted the lighting in the office, dimming the overheads and leaving just one lamp on in a corner. The action increased the sense of intimacy in a way he wouldn't have dreamed possible in his workplace. And so, with the Manhattan skyline twinkling outside the window, they dined together and sipped one of the very good bottles of red wine from his well-stocked wine racks that she'd brought to complement her cooking. And Valentin felt his desire for his wife grow by steady increments.

"I never knew you had this hidden talent for great cooking," Valentin said, toasting her with his glass. "Kudos to the chef."

"Thank you," she answered, accepting his compliment with an inclination of her head. "I surprised even myself."

"Oh, come now," he said, putting down his glass. A tendril of hair had slipped from its twist to frame her face. He reached across to gently twirl it around his forefinger. "Don't tell me you're not adept at everything you put your mind to. I know that much about

you. In that regard, you're a lot like me. Neither of us accepts failure."

He let the piece of hair drop from his finger and saw the light tremor that traveled through her as it drifted back across the responsive skin at the side of her neck. She was so sensitive to touch. Always had been. He picked up his wine again and took a generous sip. Anything to avoid touching her again and potentially breaking the spell that had surreptitiously wrapped around them in the cocoon of his office. Tonight it felt as if the rest of the world had ceased to exist—as if there were only the two of them. Oh, how he wished he could touch her. Properly touch her.

"Valentin?" Her voice had grown husky.

"Hmm?" He looked up and saw raw hunger reflected back at him. Desire punched through him and his voice was less than steady when he spoke. "Please tell me you're thinking what I'm thinking?"

A playful look stole across her face. "Well, that depends. Maybe you should tell me what you're thinking?"

"I've always preferred actions over words."

"Show me, then."

Nine

Valentin didn't need telling twice. He rose from his seat and reached for Imogene, pulling her up into his arms and against his body. Her do-me heels brought her almost to his height. She hooked her arms around his neck and her lips parted on a short intake of air.

"I didn't make dessert," she whispered. "I kind of hoped..." Her voice trailed away.

"For this?" he asked.

He took her lips with his. There was no finesse to the kiss. It was hard. It was hot. It was wet. It was everything he hoped for, wanted and needed and, judging by the way she responded in kind, it was everything she wanted, too. He could taste the red wine on her lips, her tongue, and the flavor blended with

the essential flavor of her. It was something he knew deep on an instinctive level, something he'd missed without realizing it. But she was here now. In his arms. Against his body. Heat flaring between them so they were aware only of each other.

His hands splayed across her bare back. Her skin was heated, as if she burned with a fever. He knew he burned with one. A fever for her. He reached one hand beneath the bottom edge of the dip at her lower back, lower still until he felt the bare curve of her buttocks beneath his touch. His arousal grew painfully hard as skin met skin. She'd sat there, opposite him, in that deceptively prim dress—eating dinner, sipping wine—and all the time with no underwear? Perhaps it was just as well he hadn't known or he might not have been answerable for his actions. But he planned to be answerable for them now.

His fingers flexed against the lush fullness of her, pressing her hard against his straining erection. She sighed into his mouth, running her hands through his hair, her nails scraping lightly against his scalp.

"Yes," she murmured softly. "Do that again."

She ground her hips against him as he did her bidding and cursed gently beneath her breath before she kissed him with a need that screamed how much she wanted him right now. Her tongue swept his mouth, her teeth grazed his lips, her fingers now tightened almost painfully in his hair, tugging him closer to her with each desperate mesh of their lips.

"The couch," he managed to say, pulling her with

him as he backed up toward that blessedly close piece of furniture.

He almost fell to the cushions and watched in awe as Imogene spread her legs and moved to straddle his lap. She tugged at his belt, deftly undoing his button and zipper and delving beneath his boxer briefs to release him into her hands. He groaned as her fingers closed around his length and stroked him from base to tip.

"Were you hiding this from me all through dinner?" she asked with a teasing note to her voice that made him want her all the more.

"Uh-huh."

It was all he could manage as she chose that moment to squeeze him just that little bit tighter. Sensation swamped him, making him tip his head against the back of the couch and groan again. She leaned forward and kissed him, more sweetly this time than before.

"I've missed this," she said softly against his mouth. "I've missed *you*."

He felt her shift and opened his eyes in time to watch her shimmy her dress up over her hips, exposing the cleft of skin at the apex of her thighs and the neatly trimmed thatch of dark red hair above it. She pulled the garment up over her head and let it fall behind her somewhere on the floor. Valentin's fingers ached to reach out for her, to cup her pink-tipped breasts and to roll her nipples between his fingertips. He continued to watch her as she posi-

tioned her knees on either side of him on the couch and rose up. He could feel the heat of her body as she hovered over his engorged length. If she didn't do something soon he thought he might be forced to take control. To pull her down onto him until he was buried so deeply he might never want to be separated from her again. To bury his face against her breasts and lave them with the attention they deserved. He licked his lips in anticipation.

"Uh-uh," she cautioned. "I know what you're thinking. You're about to go all he-man on me, aren't you?"

"It's under discussion with my self-control right now," he admitted.

"Well, then, you'll just have to be patient. I've forgotten one very important step."

Imogene gracefully removed herself from straddling his lap and walked, naked and still in her high heels, to her bag. He cursed himself for being an idiot the second he saw her remove a foil packet. How could he have forgotten contraception? *Because of her, that's how*, he thought, watching her walk back toward him and reassume her position. She quickly sheathed him, her touch a torment as she slid the condom over his length.

"Now, just in case you think you need to take control, I think we'll do this," she murmured as she reached for his hands and pinned them against the back of the couch. "You might be the big boss here, but right now, I'm the boss of you."

And with that she took him inside her body. Her inner muscles tightened almost unbearably around him.

"Oh."

It was all she said before she began to move, her hips tilting and rolling, lifting and dropping until all Valentin could think about was the pleasure that coiled and tightened at that point where they joined. He wouldn't have dreamed it humanly possible but he grew even harder. And try as he might, he couldn't remain an inert recipient of her attention. His hips began to thrust each time she dropped or tilted toward him. He watched her move, saw that moment her climax stole her breath and forced her to close her eyes and ride out the deep-seated rolling paroxysms of pleasure that rippled through her body. And then he saw nothing as he was gripped by his own orgasm, his body jerking and thrusting in unison with the clasp and release of hers. Satisfaction pumping from his center and through to his outer extremities.

Imogene collapsed against him, her breathing harsh, her heart racing and sweat soaking her back. Through the front of his shirt she felt the answering beat of his heart and it occurred to her that while she was completely naked, he was still essentially fully dressed. The concept made her laugh and squeeze against him.

"Well, that's a new take on the concept of office romance, isn't it?" she said lightly.

"Hey, the boss isn't complaining at all," Valentin answered as he nuzzled her neck and nipped her skin lightly with his teeth.

A shiver ran through her body, desire climbing again hard on the heels of what they'd just done together. She rocked against him and an aftershock of pleasure jolted her anew.

"It seems I can't get quite enough of you tonight," she observed, pulling away from him and reaching to loosen his tie. "And it would also seem that I dispensed with a few of the necessaries."

"Such as?"

"Such as ensuring you're as naked as I am. I want to see you, Valentin. I want to touch all of you."

"I'm yours, Imogene," he answered. His voice was deep and steady and there was a look in his eyes that promised that and so much more. "Touch me. Do whatever you want with me on one condition."

"And that is?" She paused in undoing his buttons and chewed her lower lip as she thoughtfully regarded the skin she'd already exposed on his chest.

"You allow me to do exactly what I want with you, too."

"Hmm," she said and cocked her head as if she was giving serious consideration to his words. Ridiculous, really, she thought, when he was still buried deep inside her body. She gave him another squeeze just because she could and just because she really, really wanted to. "I think that sounds reasonable."

A smile spread across his handsome face and Imo-

gene felt herself smiling back in return. Their love-making had always been impassioned but sometimes it had been fun, too. She loved that they could banter even in a situation like this.

"Does that mean I can touch you now?" Valentin growled. His eyes were hooded by half-closed lids and if anything it made him look even sexier than before.

"Please do," she said primly, and let her hands fall from his shirt.

She gasped as his palms cupped her breasts, their heat searing the sensitive undersides. His fingers and thumbs closed around the taut peaks of her nipples, squeezing them gently.

"Do you know how much I wanted to do this before?" he demanded.

"Show me," she whispered, barely capable of breathing.

The contrast between the fabric of his trousers beneath her bare legs and the warmth of his skin where he touched her was driving her to distraction. Rough and smooth, man-made and man. Everything collided together to coalesce in a feast of feeling that jumbled through her. Valentin leaned forward, his mouth closing around one nipple while he let one hand slide down to where their bodies met. His fingers brushed over her clitoris, sweeping the already oversensitized bud again and again, driving her upward toward another climax. Just before she rolled over that point and into oblivion, his teeth caught

her nipple and he bit lightly against the tender skin. It sent her flying, soaring, her body no longer her own but his to command. She was sobbing when she returned to reality, to the awareness that he'd grown hard inside her again.

And to the knowledge that they were no longer alone.

"Valentin, I have those new figures you wanted."

It was a female voice. One she recognized.

Carla Rogers.

The woman who'd wrecked their marriage. Ice-cold reality doused any lingering remnants of closeness that had existed all too briefly between her and her husband.

"Oh, I'm sorry. I didn't know you had company."

Imogene didn't mistake the vague sneer in the other woman's voice.

"Get out!" Valentin's words were clipped and vehement and laced with a fury that vibrated through him.

His arms closed around Imogene even as she tried to pull away. But he couldn't protect her from the very obvious fact that she was naked, sprawled across her husband's lap, with the tears of emotion wrought from her last orgasm still lingering on her cheeks.

"I said get out!" he repeated.

Behind them, Imogene heard a muffled apology swiftly followed by the sound of his office door closing. Imogene didn't waste any time. She yanked herself off him, bent to grab her dress off the floor

and dragged it back over her again. Shock coursed through her veins. *Carla Rogers? Here? Working with Valentin?*

Had he expected she'd never find out? Anger billowed through her, hazing her vision and twisting her mind into a dark and ugly place. She looked across the room toward the makeshift table she'd brought. To the remnants of the meal she'd so lovingly prepared. Bitterness flooded her mouth. She'd been such a bloody fool.

"It's not what you think."

Valentin had straightened his clothing and come up behind her. He rested his hands on her shoulders and started to turn her to face him.

"Don't touch me!" she spit, revulsion filling her as her mind worked overtime.

"Imogene, I can explain."

"Don't you think it's a bit late for that? Seriously, Valentin. Your old mistress? Working here? With you? How long has she been here? How long did you think you could keep that from me? Or maybe I've got it all wrong. Maybe she's not your *old* mistress after all. Maybe you never ended your affair with her." She closed her eyes and swallowed hard against the lump in her throat that threatened to choke her. When she could speak again, she opened her eyes and fixed Valentin with a fierce glare. She swept her hands out to encompass all the hard work she'd done to make the evening special for them. "Well, I hope

the two of you get a damn good laugh about all this. I'm sure you must think I'm pathetic."

"Pathetic? That's the furthest thing from what I think about you. And Carla? She's not my mistress. She wasn't seven years ago and she's not now. Believe me, Genie."

Not so much as a *please* in there, she noted as fury gripped her, leaving her shaking from head to foot.

"You want me to believe you? To trust you? That's rich," she sneered, her words dripping with revulsion and scorn. "That woman walked in on us having sex on your office couch. Have you any idea how that makes me feel? How can you possibly expect me to believe you? You had contact with her every day back then and it seems you still have contact with her every day now. Excuse me if I find it a little hard to put any confidence in what you say."

She reached for her coat and yanked it on, trying to ignore the fact that her entire body was trembling. She couldn't believe she'd been such a fool. That she'd fallen for his earnest promise back at their wedding that he'd never been unfaithful to her. She'd wanted to believe him—to believe *in* him. And all along he and his mistress had been laughing at her behind her back.

Three-month trial or not, as far as she was concerned, this marriage was well and truly on the way to being over. She headed for the door, her bag clutched in one hand. Come morning she'd contact her lawyer and see how quickly she could break the lease

and return to her brownstone. She wanted to be out from under Valentin's roof as soon as possible. And then she'd see about untangling this mess that was their marriage.

"Stop, Imogene. Don't go. Not like this."

His words came out as commands, putting her back up even more. Right now he should be groveling. Begging her forgiveness. Instead, he stood there, perfectly composed. Tall and aloof as always. And so darn handsome her heart broke all over again at his betrayal.

"Don't tell me what to do," she retorted. She made a sound of absolute disgust. "For goodness' sake, she probably even sees more of you than I do! Clearly we should have obeyed our first instincts back in Port Ludlow. Remarrying was a mistake."

"Look, I'm sorry. It came out wrong. I never lied to you about Carla. That much is true."

"But you didn't exactly rush to tell me you two continue to be work colleagues. Did she come back with you from Africa? Have you been nice and cozy together all this time?"

Even as she said the words she began to recognize them for the knee-jerk shock reaction they were. If he was so comfortable with Carla, then why had he put himself in the hands of Alice Horvath and the team at Match Made in Marriage? Why had he tried so hard to convince her to go through with their wedding when both of them hadn't initially wanted it?

Valentin's face grew bleak. "I know you won't be-

lieve me—I probably wouldn't believe me, either—but I did mean to tell you about her. When the time was right."

She barked a harsh laugh. "Right? And when would that have been, I wonder?"

Her anger, and the adrenaline that had coursed through her only moments ago, had completely faded now, replaced with overwhelming sorrow laced with exhaustion, both physical and mental.

"I'm going home," she said, dejected. "I can't deal with this right now."

"I'm taking you."

"I'll take a cab."

"I'm taking you home. No argument."

"And the food cart? We should—"

"Forget the damn food cart! I'll get someone to take care of it."

Imogene watched him as he slammed his laptop closed and shoved it in the sinfully soft leather satchel she'd bought for him only last week. Bought with love on her mind and him in her heart. She turned and stared out the window. At the sparkling skyline that had only a short time ago seemed so deliciously romantic. Again, bitterness flooded her mouth along with a deep sense of bereavement for what she thought they'd begun to build together. His voice cut through her thoughts.

"Let's go."

He stood by the door, waiting for her to come to him. His face was like granite, his posture stiff and

unyielding. It reminded her very much of the last time she'd confronted him about the ever-present Ms. Rogers. He'd rarely expressed his feelings to her without some kind of shield. The only time she'd ever felt like they'd experienced true honesty with each other was when they'd made love. But now she wondered whether even that had been just another facade after all. She buttoned up the top button of her coat and headed for the door.

Ten

The ride home was completed in utter silence. Valentin hazarded a look at Imogene but her gaze was firmly focused out the side window. When they arrived at their apartment building she didn't wait for him to come around and open her door. She was on the sidewalk and heading to the entrance of the building before he'd even said thank you and good-night to Anton. At least she'd waited for him in the elevator, he conceded to himself reluctantly.

He could feel anger and disappointment pouring off her in waves. He guessed anger was better than tears and recriminations, which was what he thought he'd be forced to bear. A flicker of irritation hovered on the edge of his mind. In fact, it was more

than irritation, it was burning up into an anger of his own. At himself. He should never have allowed a situation like that to happen. If he hadn't had the presence of mind to lock his office door, he could at least have had the presence of mind to whisk his wife home before they'd made love so they could have indulged in each other without fear of being interrupted.

His body tightened on the memory of seeing her straddle him. Of watching her strip away her dress and reveal her beautiful body to his gaze. Of hearing the sounds she made, the expression on her face.

And it had all been destroyed in a careless moment that was entirely his fault.

"I'm sorry that I put you through that," he said stiffly as the elevator car traveled to the top floor. "It was unnecessary."

She looked at him incredulously. *"Unnecessary?"* she repeated. "Your mistress walks in on us and you say it was unnecessary? Wow. You really have some gall."

The elevator doors slid open and Imogene strode into the foyer and turned immediately down the hall toward her bedroom.

"Imogene, wait. Please, we need to discuss this."

He heard her mutter, "Now he says please?"

It took her a few seconds, but she stopped and turned around.

"Honestly, Valentin. If you want this marriage to stand any chance of success—*any*—she has to go."

"Look, you're jealous, I understand that."

Imogene's face took on a scary expression as she marched back toward him. "*Jealous?* You think that's what it is? That woman deliberately destroyed our marriage seven years ago. What part of that don't you understand? Or maybe it's that you won't understand it. Maybe you can't do without her in your life. Well, I have news for you. It's her, or it's me. You cannot have us both."

"You're being childish," he responded, giving his anger a voice. "She's an integral part of Horvath Pharmaceuticals."

"Well, then, she'll have no trouble finding another job somewhere else. I'm sure you'll give her a glowing reference on all aspects of her apparently unique talents. Now, if you'll excuse me—I desperately need a shower. I feel disgusting."

She spun on one exquisitely turned heel and stalked to her room. Valentin started to follow her but realized it would be futile. Why did she have to continue to beat that old drum as far as Carla was concerned? He had no feelings for the other woman beyond those of one colleague to another. Carla had a sharp mind, and her medical background and ability to problem solve made her excellent in her role as head of research and development. And her ability to do her job well was what made their teamwork so cohesive, and that was great for Horvath Pharmaceuticals, period. It had nothing to do with

the very brief sexual relationship they'd had in Africa before Imogene even arrived on the continent.

And once she had… Well, no one else had existed for him after that. Then or since. But despite that, as he went to bed, he was left wondering if the perceived sins of the past could not be forgiven or forgotten after all.

When he rose the next morning Imogene had already left for work. Valentin was in a less-than-good mood when he went to the kitchen for his morning coffee. Dion took one look at his face and immediately poured one for him and put the mug in front of him at the breakfast bar.

"Last night not go so well?" he tentatively asked.

"The meal was fantastic. Thank you for helping Imogene organize it," Valentin managed in a civil tongue.

Dion hovered, obviously waiting in case Valentin had more to add. For a moment Valentin felt tempted to confide in the older man, who he knew had enjoyed more than forty years of marital happiness before his wife passed away, but he wasn't used to sharing personal challenges with anyone and this was more personal than most. Instead, he ate the breakfast provided to him, thanked Dion, then went on his way to work. The problems he'd been working on last night still required his urgent attention.

And his relationship with Imogene? Didn't that require his urgent attention, too? he asked himself in the car on the way to work. Of course it did, but

maybe he needed help. An impartial observer to bounce ideas off. Maybe he should call Alice and let her know she'd made a monumental mistake by matching them. But then again, things had remained strained between them and he wasn't in the mood for a lecture à la Alice. Nor, after having convinced Imogene to go ahead with the wedding a month ago, was he in the mood to admit to his grandmother that he was the one who had failed. Again. His mind rejected the idea completely. He wasn't the type to go to others for help. He solved everything himself. And he'd solve this, too.

Eventually.

Imogene fumed at her desk, furious with herself for not being able to compartmentalize her brain enough to focus on the work in front of her. She should have waited at home this morning and confronted Valentin. Cleared the air. Made her position abundantly clear as to what she wanted and expected of him. She understood that he probably didn't see an issue. It was who and how he was. She knew he didn't easily engage in relationships with people outside his immediate family. But not being prepared to let go the one person who had made Imogene's life absolute hell? That, she couldn't understand.

Last night she'd begun to feel as if they'd established a bridge between their old life and their new one. That they'd created a stable foundation upon which to move forward and to enjoy a normal marriage with

all the ups and downs that might bring. But it seemed their foundations remained weak and unstable. Built on sand ready to be washed away by the first storm to roll through and, as far as she was concerned, Carla Rogers was in the ballpark of a Category 5 hurricane.

A message pinged on her computer screen and she hastened to open it. Anything to steer her thoughts from the boiling anger that continued to distract her from what she should be doing. Her eyes widened when she saw the message and she picked up her phone and dialed through to reception.

"Send Ms. Rogers in," she managed to say in a steady voice, resisting the temptation to add, *and put security on standby in case there's a full-on fight.*

She got up from her desk and smoothed the front of her dress, glad she'd chosen severe black with a statement piece of turquoise and silver to wear around her neck. She looked formidable, which was exactly how she wanted to feel when facing her nemesis. Even so, her heart began to hammer in her chest as the door to her office opened, admitting Carla Rogers.

The woman was dressed in a two-piece ensemble that wouldn't have looked out of place on Audrey Hepburn. Her black hair was caught in a chignon and her jewelry was minimal. She looked all business, but Imogene saw the cattiness in her eyes before she composed her expression. It was clear Carla thought Imogene was no more than a mouse to be played with, then discarded at will. Well, if she thought that,

she had another think coming, Imogene decided, firming her lips and staring the other woman down.

She remained silent as she gestured for Carla to take a seat opposite her desk and waited for Carla to speak. She didn't have to wait long. After elegantly folding her legs, Carla clasped her hands on her lap and leaned forward slightly.

"I felt I needed to come and apologize," she said with what most people would assume was genuine emotion.

"Is that right?" Imogene refused to give her an inch.

Carla smiled but it failed to reach her eyes. "I'm sorry I walked in on you and Valentin last night. I wasn't expecting to find you there."

"Get to the point, Carla. We both know there's no love lost between us."

"Well, that's a shame, don't you think? We both have such strong links to Valentin. It's a shame we can't work something out like rational adults."

"So you're implying that if I don't want to share my husband with you, I'm the one being irrational?" Imogene allowed a small pitying smile to play around her lips.

"I think we can come to some arrangement. I thought he'd gotten you out of his system but it's clear he can't let either of us go."

Imogene fought the urge to leap over her desk and claw the other woman's eyes out. Instead, she leaned back in her chair, rested her elbows on the armrests

and steepled her fingers. She impaled Carla with a baleful glare. "Is that all you came here to say?"

Carla inclined her head, and for the first time some of the confidence she wore like a carapace around her began to slip.

"I'd like you leave now," Imogene stated bluntly.

"Leave? But we—"

"You've said your piece. I listened. That's all I owe you. Before you go, though, there is one thing. I will *never* share my husband with another woman. If you'd ever truly loved someone, you'd know that and feel exactly the same way. Now, do I need to call security or are you happy to leave under your own steam?"

With a sniff of annoyance, Carla rose from her chair. "You're making a mistake."

"No, *you're* making a mistake. You're assuming I'm still the same scared and insecure young woman you managed to frighten away seven years ago. Well, I have news for you. I'm not. Now, to quote my husband from last night, get out."

"This isn't over, Imogene. Don't think I'm giving up on him that easily—not after all this time."

"Giving up? Well, first of all he would have had to be invested in a relationship with you, wouldn't he? Seems to me that he wouldn't have married me, *again*—" she paused for emphasis "—if he was."

"You don't know anything," the other woman said bitterly before heading for the office door. "You'll be sorry you did this."

After she'd left, Imogene forced herself upright on legs that shook with the aftermath of emotion and headed out to her next meeting. She wasn't sure how she managed to get through the rest of her day, but by the time she'd picked up her laptop case and headed out the office she'd achieved a lot. Maybe she should run on a postconfrontation anger-adrenaline high more often, she told herself as she headed downstairs and hailed a cab. While she'd been in a mild state of shock after Carla left, she felt incredibly empowered. For the first time she felt like she'd taken the upper hand and held on to it, and she was proud of herself for that. Whether Valentin would be so proud was another thing. He'd better not be working late tonight, she quietly seethed, or she'd have no hesitation in bowling up to him at work and having this out there.

It turned out she needn't have worried. He was already home when she entered the apartment, and working in the library. She walked straight in and waited for him to look up.

"I had a visitor today," she began.

"Clearly they did not improve your mood," he observed dryly.

"No, never let it be said that Carla Rogers improves anything," she replied.

She was rewarded with a look of shock on his face.

"Carla came to see you today? I didn't expect that."

"Nor did I, but yes. She said she came to apologize.

But then she got to her real agenda. She thought it might be nice if we came to some agreement together."

"An agreement. That sounds reasonable," he said with caution.

"Whereby we *share* you," Imogene enunciated clearly.

The look of shock hardened to granite. "And you said?"

"I told her I didn't share my husband with anyone."

His eyes gleamed; he looked impressed and not a little relieved. "Well, I'm pleased to hear it."

"You don't understand, Valentin. She seems to think she has rights to you and that it's okay to bully me. I set her straight on both counts. However, if you don't support me in this, whatever I say won't carry any weight. She's vicious and she's manipulative. She tore us apart once before and she will do anything in her power to do it again.

"You need to believe me. I said it last night and I'll say it again. Either she goes, or I will. I will not have a ménage marriage."

"I'm not suggesting anything of the kind. I want this to work as much as you do." He got up from his desk and crossed the floor toward her to take her hands in his. "Imogene, last night was incredibly special to me. *You* are incredibly special to me. I want this to be forever."

She tugged her hands free. "Words are easy enough to say, Valentin. It's action I need to see. I don't want her working with you. That's it."

"So my promise to you, to remain faithful only unto you—that isn't enough?"

Imogene only wished it were. She knew that he saw her as unnecessarily obsessed with the other woman but was it too much to ask him to see things from her side?

"Not when she's around."

"So you expect me to let go a member of staff who is not only a valuable team leader but instrumental in the current talks we're having for a global supply contract with an international aid organization."

Imogene held her ground and nodded. "I most certainly do."

"Even if I told you that I love you? That I've only ever loved you?"

Eleven

She stood there in shock. She'd wished to hear those words from his lips again, but had feared it would never happen. And now, while they were fighting over someone else, he threw them into the conversation, just like that? She didn't know what to do. She'd imagined when they exchanged these words it would be over something special, something meaningful to them both. Not that they'd be used as ammunition so he didn't have to disrupt the impeccably smooth running of his workplace. She blinked back unexpected tears.

"That's not fair. You can't use love against me like that," she said in a voice that was barely above a whisper.

"Not fair? It's the truth. I've always loved you, Imogene. Remarrying you has only served to underscore that for me all over again. I don't want anyone else. Only you. Always you."

Imogene felt as if her chest were being torn open. She would have given anything for these words seven years ago. She would have had the strength to stay and fight for her husband, for their marriage, instead of running away. But she was the one who'd found Carla in her bed while someone showered in their bathroom. She'd assumed it was Valentin and, shouldering all the deeply embedded damage of a child of an unfaithful parent, she'd run from the hurt and injustice of what she thought she'd seen.

A month ago, at their wedding, he'd emphatically reiterated to her that the person in the bathroom hadn't been him, and she'd wanted so much to believe him. To believe they had a second chance. But if he was being honest and he truly thought he loved her, then it wasn't enough. He needed to show her this time. To prove he meant it. She would settle for absolutely nothing less.

Valentin lifted one hand to her face and gently cupped her cheek, forcing her to look directly at him. "Imogene, I mean every word. But if we are to make this work, you have to trust me. I have no feelings for Carla other than the respect of one colleague for another—that's basically all there has ever been between us. I can't jeopardize everything we've been

working for by releasing her from her employment contract right now."

His touch was tender but his words were like bullets to her soul.

"So basically you're telling me you're not prepared to do anything," she said, fighting to keep her voice even.

"I will talk to her tomorrow. Discuss what you've told me."

Imogene pulled away from him. "Discuss all you want. It won't change a thing as far as she's concerned. And until you can see that, too, we don't stand a chance." She started to head out the library but then stopped in the doorway. "Valentin, tell me this. What do you think she stood to gain when, back in Africa, she one hundred percent led me to believe it was you in the bathroom showering off the sweat of your lovemaking with her? Why would she have lied about that then if it wasn't her intention all along to have you to herself? Anyone else would have given up and moved on when we married for a second time, but for some reason she can't let you go. Carla Rogers is a predator and she has you very firmly in her sights. If you can't see that, then I'm sorry but you must be completely blind."

Valentin rubbed at his eyes. He'd endured another sleepless night, in the end going into the home gym and pounding out some miles on the treadmill to wear himself out. With every stride, one question

continued to repeat in his head and had been there again at the forefront of his thoughts on waking. Why wasn't his love enough for Imogene? Maybe she was right after all. Maybe they didn't have a future together. As far as he saw it he was doing everything reasonably possible to rebuild their relationship, but her preoccupation with Carla Rogers made her appear slightly unhinged. So he was going to the source—Carla Rogers—who would be here in his office at any moment.

A sound at the door made him turn away from the window.

"You wanted to see me?" Carla said as she walked toward his desk.

She looked, as ever, perfectly composed. He'd seen this woman in the most dire and urgent of trauma circumstances when a gang war had blown up in the African city they'd been assigned to work in, and through all the blood and the chaos she'd been a rock of calm and reason. She was, like him, a person dedicated to their work, whether it be a hands-on situation like multiple patients with horrendous injuries or the development of a new product that would have far-reaching implications in developing countries. He'd come to rely on her—then as much as now—and he couldn't see his working life without her. Correction, he didn't want to see his working life without her, a voice that sounded suspiciously like Imogene's chided in his head. He pushed the thought aside and smiled at Carla.

"Thank you for coming. I know you're busy."

"I always have time for you, Valentin. You know that."

He hated that he suddenly couldn't take her words at face value. That the things Imogene had said to him last night, and the night before, made him twist what Carla said and look at it from a different angle. Did she have another agenda? Was that innuendo in her tone? He looked carefully at her perfectly made-up face and into the dark eyes that were the window to her brilliant mind, and saw nothing but the familiar features he'd known now for more than eight years. He sucked in a deep breath and chose his words carefully. No point in sugarcoating them. Carla was the kind of woman who came straight to the point, and he owed it to her to be equally up-front.

"I understand you went to visit Imogene at her office yesterday," he started.

To his surprise, Carla laughed.

"Oh, so she told you about that, did she?"

"Did you expect she wouldn't? We don't keep secrets from each other."

"Oh, I don't expect you think you do."

He was affronted by her choice of words. "What do you mean by that?"

"I suppose she told you I surprised her with my visit." Carla paused, looking at him for a response. When none was forthcoming, she carried on. "She summoned me to her office. I was quite surprised. But she's your wife, and even though it took me away

from precious hours here at work, I thought it must be important. So I went. I have to say, I was shocked. She was extremely rude to me. Told me I should start looking for another job because she didn't want me anywhere near you. It's ridiculous really, when we both know you have no possible grounds to rescind my employment contract. Your wife has a serious problem with jealousy, Valentin. She acted crazy. And to think she's involved in the childcare indus-try? It's all bit scary, to be honest."

Valentin hid his shock with a great deal of effort. Which woman was telling the truth? The behavior Carla had described didn't sound like the Imogene he knew, but then again, how well did he really know her? Their first marriage had been conducted after only a few short weeks of knowing each other. And those weeks had been driven by lust and passion and a heightened sense of drama in a city that was under constant threat. It had hardly been a normal court-ship. And nor had their marriage been, either. The time they'd managed to spend together was short and sweet, and there'd been little room for long and meaningful discussions. Not when they couldn't keep their hands off each other. Until Imogene had be-lieved he'd rekindled his relationship with Carla. At that point, yes, she'd been unreasonable.

His heart told him he needed to believe his wife, but logic—his fallback in any situation—told him to stand by his employee. Someone he'd worked with and whom he trusted implicitly. Neither answer sat

comfortably on his shoulders but there had to be a middle ground there somewhere. Surely.

"It's not the story she gave you, is it?" Carla asked with one arched brow.

"There are some differences, yes," he reluctantly admitted. "I will discuss it with her further."

"Don't bother. Honestly, if you were my husband and the situation were reversed, I'd probably be staking my claim, too."

There was a note of truth that rang loud and clear in her words.

"Staking your claim?" He forced a laugh. "Kind of makes it sound like I don't have a choice in all this. I have to say, I feel a bit like a bone caught between two dogs."

"Don't you mean two bitches?" Carla asked impishly.

This time his humor didn't have to be forced. "Well, since you put it that way. Not that either of you are, of course."

"Of course not," Carla all but purred.

For some reason, her manner brushed his nerves the wrong way. Like fingers running against a velvet pile.

"Now that I have you here, let's finalize the budget predictions we've been working on," he said, determined to change the subject.

In an instant she was all business, something he was grateful for, because throughout their discussion he'd found himself wanting to believe her, yet not quite managing to. Could it be that Imogene had

told him the truth, or had it simply been her version of the truth? Somehow, he had to figure it out.

That night Valentin made certain he was home on time because they were expected for dinner at Imogene's parents' house. After a day mulling over what Imogene and Carla had said, he was no closer to working out which woman had given him the real turn of events in Imogene's office, and things remained strained between him and his wife as they were driven to her parents' apartment building.

"You didn't tell me your mom and dad lived so close to us," Valentin commented as they pulled up at the prestigious Fifth Avenue address.

Imogene merely shrugged. "Is it important?"

"They are your parents."

"Yes, but we don't spend a lot of time together. Dad's always busy. Mom, too."

"Your dad's a human rights lawyer, isn't he?"

"Yes, one of the best. It puts him in demand. So much so, I'm surprised tonight wasn't postponed, like things like this usually are."

Valentin heard a note of weary resignation in her voice that pricked at him unexpectedly. In their first marriage he'd rarely been home when he said he would. Every day, emergencies had arisen that had required his immediate attention. His, or his ego's? a little voice asked from the back of his mind. He had been part of a team. Not the only trauma surgeon in the hospital. And always on call if he'd been needed.

But he had to admit, he'd enjoyed the urgency of the ER. Excelled under the pressure of time-sensitive situations. A lot of people accused surgeons of having a God complex, but the truth was they did literally hold the life of another human being in their hands at times. It had been an adrenaline rush, he couldn't deny it. And he'd loved his work wholeheartedly. Still did, although what he did now was so different.

As much as he professed to love his wife?

It was not the same, he argued internally as they entered the building on Fifth and took the elevator to her parents' apartment. Beside him, he felt Imogene stiffen.

"Everything okay?"

"About as okay as it gets, I suppose."

She appeared to brace herself as the elevator doors slid open and they walked together down the paneled hall to a set of wooden double doors. She'd no sooner pressed the buzzer than her mother swung the door open for them. Caroline O'Connor was a beautiful woman. In her early fifties, she clearly had been able to enjoy the best of everything when it came to personal grooming. Her hair was a few shades lighter than her daughter's, but her clear gray-green eyes were the same.

"Mrs. O'Connor," Valentin said, as they entered the vestibule and he put out his hand. "It's a pleasure to see you again."

"Oh, I don't think we need to stand on ceremony, do you?" The older woman gave him a smile and,

ignoring his outstretched hand, reached up to plant a swift kiss near his cheek. "After all, we're family now. Call me Caroline, please."

"Caroline," he repeated with a quick smile.

"Is Dad home yet?" Imogene asked, looking past her mother into the large empty sitting room beyond.

"Not yet. There's been a little holdup. You know what he's like," her mother said smoothly but with a look of censure at her daughter.

Imogene ignored the silent caution. "Honestly, Mom, he could have made an effort for us. It's the first time he's getting to meet Valentin. Anyone would think he didn't care we've gotten married."

Caroline started to protest but Valentin stepped smoothly in, touching Imogene on the shoulder. "Don't worry. I know what it's like when you get caught up at work."

"Yes, you do, don't you?" Imogene said pointedly before stepping away and shrugging off her coat to hang it in a cupboard off to one side.

Valentin bit back the retort that sprang to his lips. He wasn't going to point out to his wife that lately she'd been home at erratic hours herself and he certainly wasn't going to enter into a debate in front of her mother. Caroline stood looking from her daughter to him and back again, a small worried frown creasing her almost impossibly smooth brow.

"You have a lovely home," Valentin said to her in an attempt to break the growing tension. "Have you lived here long?"

"Our entire married life," Caroline said with an ease he was sure was well practiced. "When Howard and I moved in here we only had this floor, but when another apartment came available above us, he bought that also and converted this into a duplex. Would you like me to show you around? Dinner won't be for another hour. We'll still have time for a nice drink before we dine."

Valentin looked across at Imogene, who shrugged again much as she'd done in the elevator before. "Do what you want," she said. "I'm going to check on what Susan's preparing for us."

The tour of the seven-bedroom apartment took longer than he expected, or maybe it was just because Caroline was very clearly stalling to mask the absence of her husband. By the time they returned to the sitting room, Imogene was seated in one of the expensively upholstered easy chairs with an almost empty glass of wine in her hand.

"I was beginning to think I'd have to send out a search party," she said, rising to her feet. "Shall I get you each a drink?"

"Thank you, darling," her mother said, allowing Imogene to assume hostess duties.

Once their aperitifs were finished a uniformed maid called them to the dining room. Still no sign of Mr. O'Connor, Valentin noted with sympathy for his new mother-in-law, who'd done her best to fill the void left by her husband by steering the conversation seamlessly before dinner. They'd just begun

their appetizers when the sound of the front door banging shut echoed through the apartment.

In moments the energy of the room changed with both women sitting just a little straighter. There was an expression of hopeful relief on Caroline's face and one of annoyance on her daughter's.

"Be nice," Caroline had time to hiss across the table to Imogene before Howard O'Connor entered the room.

"Sorry I'm late, people. Couldn't be avoided. I'm sorry. You must be my new son-in-law," he said smoothly, as if meeting the man his only daughter had married was a frequent occurrence. Valentin stood and offered his hand. "Or should I say recycled son-in-law," Howard added with a hearty laugh at his own attempt at humor.

Valentin tried not to bristle. For someone who ought to be adept at diplomacy, the man was trying far too hard. "It's good to meet you at last, sir."

"And you, Horvath. And you."

Howard turned his attention to Imogene, who sat quietly at the table, but not before Valentin noticed a lingering hint of a woman's fragrance around his host. His nostrils flared as he analyzed it and came to a rapid conclusion. He'd smelled the subtle scent Caroline O'Connor wore as she'd shown him around the apartment. This was entirely different. The man had obviously not been tied up at work—unless work entailed being in very close, possibly intimate, contact with another woman. At the table, Caroline laughed

brittlely at something her husband said, her eyes not leaving him for a second. Her daughter, on the other hand, stared at her plate.

Was that what lay behind Imogene's insecurity around him? Was Howard O'Connor an unfaithful husband and all-too-absent father? Suddenly Imogene's obsession with fidelity and her issues with trust were coming into very clear focus indeed.

Twelve

They'd just had their main dishes brought to the table when Howard's cell phone began to chime insistently. Excusing himself, he rose from his chair and left the room. Valentin heard his voice recede down the hallway, then grow more muffled as he closed a door behind him.

"Sorry about that," Caroline said. "We've had to learn to share him with his work. Well, it's more of a vocation, really. A calling. You must feel the same with your medical background, Valentin."

Valentin looked across at Imogene, who stared evenly back at him. He could usually read his wife, who was becoming accustomed to the nuances in her expression. But right now she was a blank canvas.

"I don't know why you keep apologizing for him, Mom," she said, not taking her eyes from Valentin's. "You know we play second fiddle to Dad's other... interests."

The words were crushing but Valentin could hear the pain behind them. And the warning. She'd grown up with this. She was not going to tolerate it in her own marriage. Dessert became an exercise in diplomacy as Valentin attempted to temper his wife's darkening mood with her mother's overeager attempts to cover the glaring absence of her husband. It was a relief when it was all over.

By the time they returned home, Valentin knew they had to talk this out before it grew into a black hole between them.

"Have you got time for a nightcap?" he asked as he helped her out of her coat. "I'd like to talk."

"I thought you might," she said. "Make mine a brandy. I think I'm going to need it."

There was an attitude about her now, as if nothing and no one could break her. But he knew only too well how fragile she was and how shaky the barriers she'd erected around her.

"Brandy it is," he agreed.

By silent mutual consent they went into the library and Valentin poured them each a measure of brandy before joining her on the sofa.

"That was a tough night for you," he said without preamble.

"You think that was tough? Sadly, that was nor-

mal. At least, that's what my mother thinks. I don't know why she puts up with it." She shook her head before taking a sip of her drink. "No, that's not true. I know exactly why she puts up with it. I don't think she loves my father any more than he loves her. They both, however, love the illusion of a stable marriage and the lifestyle my father's income allows them to enjoy."

She sounded so bitter. So damaged. It made his chest ache to hear her speak that way. He decided to get straight to the point. "Has your father always been unfaithful?"

She looked at him and raised her brows. "You noticed that already, did you?"

"Well, kind of hard not to when he came home smelling of some other woman's perfume."

"He used to shower before coming home. Now he doesn't care enough to hide it. Mom just turns the other cheek. She's fought long and hard for her position in society and her home. She's not about to rock that boat for the sake of his mistress of the hour."

What kind of upbringing had Imogene had for this kind of behavior to be so accepted, so normal? He felt sorry for her having had to grow up with that. His own father had been a workaholic but he'd loved his wife fiercely and protected what family time he could carve out.

"I'm sorry, Imogene. You deserve better."

"Yes, I do," she agreed emphatically. "Look, it might be a situation that my mother is happy to toler-

ate, but I've seen what it's done to her over the years. She might have loved my father in the beginning, but bit by bit that's slowly died. When something isn't nurtured, shared and encouraged, what else can it do? They have nothing in common anymore aside from their desire to present the perfect facade to the world. Mom acts as hostess when he entertains foreign visitors and he acts the devoted husband when anybody else is watching."

"He was hardly the devoted husband this evening," Valentin felt obliged to point out.

"That's because he stands to gain nothing from his association with you. You're merely my husband, and in my father's eyes his family comes a very solid last in any bid for his attention. I learned that from the cradle, Valentin. I will not subject my children to the same thing."

The warning in her voice was loud and clear.

"I will be here for our children, Imogene. And for you."

"You're making the assumption that our marriage will last."

He bristled slightly. "There's no reason why it won't."

"There is one," she answered sharply. "One you either won't see, or refuse to admit to."

"Look, let me make it absolutely clear to you. I am not your father. I'm nothing like him. I am and have always been faithful to you. I know you believe you saw evidence to the contrary and I know

you were left hurt and bewildered. I acted selfishly when we were in Africa. I put my work ahead of you because I didn't realize how tenuous our relationship was. That was my fault. Giving Carla the keys to our place so she could sleep was my fault. I had no idea she'd use the opportunity for some tryst and I'm sorry you were led to believe I was involved in that tryst. I don't know how much more often I have to tell you that before you believe me."

Imogene stared into his eyes, her face softening. "I want to believe you, Valentin. If I didn't think I could believe you I wouldn't have married you. But she's still in your life. Still making trouble between us. As long as she's there, there will always be trouble. Can't you see that? Look, my father has had several mistresses during his marriage to my mom. Because he doesn't love them, he doesn't see that as being unfaithful. In fact, he's convinced himself that he's not. But fidelity is everything to me. *Everything.*"

"You have my promise, Imogene. There is no one else but you for me. I really want you to believe that. I love you and I want a life with you, children with you."

"Like I said, I want to believe you, Valentin—" she began.

"Then believe me. That's all it takes," he urged.

"I wish it were as simple as that."

"We can make it that simple."

He reached across and took her glass from her

and put it on the coffee table beside his own. Then, cupping her face gently, he kissed her. There was no heat in the kiss, nothing like the passion that had overwhelmed them the other night. Nothing but a steadfast reassurance that he was here for her. Her man. No one else's. Her lips trembled beneath his, parting as his tongue traced the fullness of them. As he ended the kiss and pulled back, he looked into her eyes and made a silent promise. Come what may, he would convince her of his love for her. They would succeed on this rocky journey of theirs and they'd come out stronger at the end as a result of it.

He got to his feet, holding out a hand to her. "Sleep with me tonight."

"I don't know, Valentin."

"Just sleep. Nothing more. I want you in my arms, in my bed. With me and beside me."

"Okay," she agreed.

She took his hand and together they walked down the hallway to the master suite. While she used the bathroom, he turned down the bed, and on her return he helped her undress.

"Hop into bed, I'll only be a minute," he said, heading for the bathroom himself.

He heard the rustle of the sheets as she did as he suggested. When he returned to the bedroom she was lying back on a pillow, sheets tucked up to her chin and her body rigid with tension. He shucked off his clothes and slid into the bed beside her, reaching for her and pulling her against him. He pressed

a kiss against her nape, inhaling the scent of her hair, her skin.

"Good night, Imogene. We'll work this out."

She didn't respond and for a while he began to wonder if she would, but then he heard a softly uttered "G'night."

He smiled in the darkness. He understood now why she was so adamant about the situation with Carla. After what had happened in Africa and with her own father's less-than-stellar example, Imogene felt vulnerable. Afraid to trust. Well, he had to earn that back from her—somehow, someway. He felt her begin to relax incrementally in his arms and listened as her breathing slowed until she was finally asleep.

Valentin lay there for ages, wondering if she'd ever feel secure with him. She said she wanted to believe him but in light of the conditioning she'd had growing up, could she ever really trust anyone? He hoped so, because he wasn't fooling himself about fidelity like Howard O'Connor was. But given how Imogene felt, could she be rational about the subject? Their first attempt at marriage had been anything but rational, and now, thinking about it, he was reminded of the conversation he'd had with Carla earlier today and of what she'd said about Imogene. Tonight had hardly been the time to bring that up with his wife, but how on earth was he going to get to the root of the issue without discussing it with her?

If he could be certain Carla was the one who lied, then he would obviously not be able to trust her again.

It would be much easier to insist on her exit from Horvath Pharmaceuticals. But if she'd been telling the truth...what then?

Imogene woke the next morning to find herself alone in bed. In Valentin's bed, she realized sleepily. She hadn't slept that deeply in a long time. She stretched out, then started in surprise as Valentin strode naked from the bathroom. Her eyes hungrily roamed his body. For someone who put in long hours in what was essentially a sedentary job, he still managed to find time to work out. His body was beautiful, from the breadth of his powerful shoulders all the way past his hips and lower. She felt her mouth go dry and swallowed, hard.

"Good morning," he said with a smile that told her he hadn't missed her detailed perusal of his body and that he also didn't mind one little bit. "Sleep well?"

"Really well, thank you."

She struggled to sit up against the pillows and tugged the bedsheets up with her.

"Don't bother on my account," he teased as he walked to an antique tallboy and pulled out a drawer.

A flush of color heated her cheeks at his words. They were hardly strangers to each other and yet she felt uncomfortable being naked in front of him this morning, as if it left her feeling too exposed. In light of their conversation last night, it was no wonder. She'd shared truths with him she'd never shared with anyone else. Growing up, all her friends had

envied her the fact her parents had the perfect marriage. It was an ironic analogy, she thought, that here she was, hiding beneath the sheets, much as she hid so much of herself, while her husband strode confident and naked about the bedroom. Could she take that to mean that he was being as open and honest about everything, his feelings for her included, as he was with his body?

"Which one?" Valentin said abruptly, turning to face her and holding a silk tie in each hand.

For a second her mind wandered, thinking of a suggestion she could make to him for using both ties, but she quickly pushed it away. "Depends on your suit, I guess. And your shirt."

"Navy and plain white."

"Then the red and navy broad stripes."

"Thanks."

With that he pushed the other tie back in the drawer and went through to the bathroom. She heard the dressing room door on the other side of the bathroom close. Imogene lay back in the bed and realized her heart was racing. What had just happened? Their exchange had been so normal and yet here she was as nervous as a mouse in a room full of cats. She got up from the bed and wrapped the sheet around her before picking up her clothes and heading down the hall to her bedroom. After a quick shower and getting dressed in a tailored pantsuit for work, she went through to the kitchen. Valentin was already there, sipping his coffee at the breakfast bar.

"I'll be late home tonight. My new CEO is shadowing me for the day and we're visiting our New York centers before spending the rest of the afternoon in the office."

"Thanks for the heads-up," Valentin replied before getting up and taking his cup to the sink. "I'll wait up for you."

"You don't need to do that," she said. "I don't know how late I'll be."

"Yes, I do. I'll see you tonight."

He kissed her on the lips, hard and swift, and then he was gone. Imogene stared in his wake, wondering what the heck had just happened. She was interrupted by Dion coming through from the butler's pantry.

"An omelet this morning, Mrs. Horvath?"

"No, thank you, Dion. Just coffee this morning."

He tsk-tsked under his breath as he poured her coffee with cream, just the way she liked it. She downed the coffee, only barely tasting it, then collected her computer case and headed out the door.

She was early to the office but even so her new CEO had beaten her in. She smiled as she walked toward him, knowing that the board of directors had made an excellent choice in Eric Grafton. A Columbia graduate, he'd gained a strong reputation across a range of businesses—every last one of them becoming more successful than they'd been before he took charge. She couldn't complain about that. And he was a genuinely nice guy. Married to his high

school sweetheart, with two daughters of his own, he seemed to have found the perfect balance between life and career. She envied him that, she realized.

"Eric, good to see you," she said, walking toward him with her hand outstretched.

His clasp was warm and strong, much like the image he portrayed.

As they discussed their plans for the weeks ahead her mind kept drifting back to Valentin and last night. It had been comforting to sleep in his arms and had given her hope they were on the right track together. They had better be, she thought as she glanced at the man who was taking over her role here in the company she'd created. In this, at least, she was confident she was leaving her business in good hands. If only she could be as confident about her private life.

The next few weeks became a blur of center visits across the country, traveling with Eric and introducing him to the franchise holders nationwide. She hated being away from Valentin, but it couldn't be avoided. They hadn't slept together again since that night after dinner at her parents', and she found herself missing him at unexpected moments. Still, it wouldn't be for much longer, she told herself. Once she was back in the classroom her hours would be more regular.

And the three-month trial period of their marriage would be looming, she realized. The thought of walking away from Valentin made her feel physically ill, but as far as she was aware he was still working

with Carla. Of course she understood that if he was to let the other woman go, there would have to be an exit strategy. As much as she disliked and distrusted Carla, she knew she couldn't simply be turned out of her job and onto the streets. Due process needed to be followed. But was Valentin even doing anything about it, or was he simply allowing things to continue as they had before? She knew she needed to discuss it with him, but the opportunity hadn't arisen and with her hours lately they'd become ships in the night. Much like they had in the early days of their marriage before she'd taken the bull by the horns and taken dinner to him in his office.

She made an involuntary sound as her body clenched tight in response to the memory of that night.

"Everything okay?" Eric asked from beside her in the cab as they headed from the airport back to their office.

"Fine, thanks," she managed smoothly.

It was hard to think about that night without thinking about what had happened next. And her confrontation with Valentin over Carla. They remained at an impasse and she didn't like it one bit. She was going to have a make a decision in the next few weeks, whether she liked it or not. Stay, and potentially put herself in the same position her mother lived in—because she had no doubt that Carla Rogers would not retract her claws from what she saw as her proprietary interest in Valentin—or walk away.

Imogene felt her stomach flip uncomfortably as she accepted that if she was to be true to herself, she really only had one option, and it just about broke her heart to admit it.

example, but the manual. The unusual considering the occupied and if she wasn't be unable to quick and if say many to done reason, and if just as dead to must be been to exhibit is

Thirteen

He missed her.

Seeing Imogene work such long hours, coming home late at night and worn-out, gave him a new appreciation for how hard she worked and also reminded him of what she'd had to put up with from him in the early days of their marriage. He didn't like it, not one bit, but having some understanding of what she had gone through made him vow to strive to keep more regular hours at the office, and to encourage his staff to do the same. But on a personal basis, the days of separation were creating their own issues—widening the gulf that had developed between them even further. They didn't even have an opportunity to talk to each other beyond the basics of

common courtesy. They'd gone from trying to build a marriage to living like a pair of roommates and it made him feel a difficult combination of emotions. He, who had always been the calm in a storm, had become short-tempered at work and taciturn here at home. Even with Dion, who had done nothing wrong, Valentin had snapped unnecessarily—like when he'd very reasonably asked him if Imogene would be home for dinner.

He walked over to the window overlooking the park and took in a deep breath. This unreasonable, moody behavior wasn't him. Worse, he knew precisely why he was behaving this way. He was afraid his marriage was dying before it even had a chance to live. He had to do something, but what? How did a man woo back his woman when they barely spent any time together?

Make time for each other, a little voice in the back of his head prodded him none too gently. A light bulb went off. She'd brought him dinner at work when he was working late; the least he could do for her was the very same thing.

"Dion!" he shouted as he strode out of his office.

"Yes, Mr. Horvath?" Dion said, wiping his hands on an apron as he came into the hall from the kitchen.

"First, I need to apologize to you for being a bear this evening...well, every evening these past few weeks."

"That's all right, sir. I know you're missing Mrs. Horvath."

"You do?"

"Of course, it's only natural. She's missing you, too. But if you'll excuse me for being forward, neither of you seem to know what to do about it."

"You're right," Valentin agreed. "We've been married before, to each other, and it all blew up in our faces. Now I think we're both too wary to fully commit again."

"Understandable, sir. No one enters into these things expecting or wanting to be hurt again. But love brings vulnerability and at a certain point you need to surrender to that to give love a chance."

His words sank deep. "You're very wise, Dion. You must miss your wife a lot."

"With every breath, sir. Now, what else was it that you wanted?"

"I thought I might return the favor to Imogene and take dinner to her at work."

A large smile split Dion's lined face. "That's an excellent idea, sir. I'll get on it straightaway."

Dion was as good as his word. Within an hour he had a fragrant meal of spaghetti Bolognese together with salad and a wrapped loaf of warm, fresh bread.

"Did you want to use the trolley, sir, or the thermal picnic pack?"

Valentin thought about the night Imogene had brought dinner to him and how special it had been dining by his office window. But this time he wanted to make it different, and hopefully achieve an ending that was far less traumatic than the last one had been.

"No, I think I'll just wing it and use the pack, but perhaps take a tablecloth or blanket, as well?"

"I have just the things, sir."

Fifteen minutes later Valentin was in the elevator of Imogene's building and heading to her floor. The doors pinged open, revealing a large open-plan office space with several individual offices lining the outside edge. Not a soul was around, and most of the lighting was dimmed, but over in a far corner, Valentin made out a glow of light. He struck out toward it, realizing he really should have shown more interest in Imogene's work and workplace before now. In fact, coming here, not knowing exactly where he was going, was like holding up a mirror to how he'd been treating his marriage so far. He had to do better. All along he'd been saying he was invested in making their union work when he'd really only been going through the motions, not taking an active part in making things work. He'd slid back into his old habits and had made few changes to his life to accommodate the fact that he was, once again, married.

With the promise of doing better echoing in his mind, he reached the door of the lit office and looked inside. Two heads were bent close together at the large desk over by the window. Very close together. Suddenly Valentin had an all-too-vivid realization of what Imogene had been going through with him continuing to work with Carla, because a vicious surge of jealousy cut through him like a hot knife through butter. He must have made some kind of noise because

simultaneously, the two heads looked up and straight at him. Imogene seemed at first shocked, then over-joyed to see him there.

"Valentin, this is a lovely surprise," she said, coming around from the desk and walking quickly toward him.

But when she reached him, she hesitated, as if unsure of what she ought to do next. Given the estrangement they were suffering, it was no wonder, he told himself, and he put down the pack and reached for her, kissing her on the cheek briefly before letting her go.

"I thought I'd bring you dinner," he said, looking straight into her eyes and trying to tell her with so many words unsaid that he was doing his best to take steps to rebuild the bridge that had broken down between them.

"That's so thoughtful of you. Eric and I were just saying we needed to finish what we were doing. Eric, come and meet my husband."

She gestured to the man, now standing beside her desk, and he came forward, hand outstretched. Valentin did his best to remain courteous but it wasn't easy. This was the man Imogene had been spending hours with, traveling overnight with. A man she'd been spending more time with than she'd been spending at home. It was hard not to feel some pangs of envy, especially when they were obviously already close.

"Your wife is quite a woman," Eric said after

their initial introductions had been performed. "I'm stunned by what she's achieved with her business and honored I was chosen to fill her shoes as CEO."

"She's quite a woman, all right," Valentin agreed, silently adding, *my woman*.

Eric seemed to pick up on the invisible tension and turned to Imogene. "I'll leave you to it and we can get back to work in the morning. My wife and girls will be waiting for me."

He added the last with a pointed look at Valentin, as if assuring him that he wasn't poaching on his property in any way. Valentin gave him a short nod in acknowledgment.

"Thanks, Eric," Imogene said, looking from one man to the other as if realizing she'd just missed some kind of silent male communication between them.

Once Eric was gone Imogene turned to face Valentin. "What the heck was that all about?"

"You never told me your new CEO is tall, dark, handsome and charming," he said before he could stop himself.

To his surprise, Imogene laughed. "You're kidding me, right? He's also married and a devoted father and not interested in me in that way at all. In fact, he's been a breath of fresh air because he doesn't see me purely as a woman but as a business equal."

Valentin reached for her again, encircling her in his arms. "He doesn't see you as a woman? Then

there is something very seriously wrong with him because you're beautiful."

He bent his head and captured her lips before she could speak and in that brief instant he knew he'd done the right thing in coming here tonight. He needed this, but more than that, he needed her to know—to be sure—that he was here for her, for them. He ended the kiss and reluctantly released her.

"Are you hungry?" he asked, bending to retrieve the picnic pack from the floor.

"Starving. I can't remember when I last ate."

Valentin tsk-tsked under his breath. "You need to look after yourself better," he said, then stopped and corrected himself. "No, *I* need to look after you better."

"I'm a grown woman, Valentin. I can look after myself."

"But that's the thing," he said. "You don't need to do it all yourself. I'm here for you."

"Are you?" she asked, a wary look in her eyes. "I know you're here now, but are you really there for me 24/7?"

She had every right to ask that question. He knew that. And in all honesty, he couldn't tell her he had been.

"Look, we both have work to do in our relationship. You need to trust me but more than that, I need to make it clearer to you that you can." He sucked in a harsh breath and decided to come out with com-

plete honesty. "I hated seeing you here with Eric like that this evening."

"Valen—"

"No, please, hear me out. I refused to understand how you felt about Carla, and that's on me. I've been an idiot. It wasn't until the shoe was on the other foot that I began to get an inkling as to how you've been feeling all this time."

A frown drew lines on her forehead and her eyes reflected her concern. "I don't think you can understand, Valentin. Seeing me working with my replacement, a man who won't be a big part of my life once I've fully stepped down, is nothing compared to you continuing to work with a woman you once were intimate with. A woman who is doing her best to undermine me."

Valentin swallowed. She was right. If Eric had been a part of her past, Valentin would likely have stepped into her office and then engaged in a very unattractive brawl right here with her new CEO. Some Neanderthal part of his brain had gone into overdrive when he'd seen the two of them together, quite without reason. But then reason always had fled when it came to him and Imogene, hadn't it?

"You're right," he said, swallowing the last of his pride. "I may not ever understand fully how much I've hurt you, but I want it to be clear that I never want to hurt you like that ever again. I'll be talking to the Horvath legal department in the morning to see what I can do in terms of letting Carla go or

moving her to another office away from New York. Beyond all else, you are the most important person to me and your happiness is my goal."

He saw tears swim in her eyes before pooling and spilling down her cheeks. If she'd cut him with a knife it couldn't have hurt any more than realizing just how much this meant to her and how little attention he'd really paid to it. He'd assumed she was jealous, and, yes, she probably was, but she'd had a valid point. And he'd ignored that, putting his company's interests ahead of his wife's.

"I love you, Imogene. Believe me."

"I believe you," she whispered.

He kissed her again, pulling her close to his body where she fitted against him so perfectly. Their embrace was tender, an affirmation of their commitment to each other. When they parted, Valentin felt like they had forged a new link between them. One that was stronger than before, one that would stand the test of time.

Imogene looked at her husband, seeing his sincerity and feeling a new sense of hope fill the dark empty place that had taken up residence where her heart should be ever since Carla Rogers had walked in on them weeks ago. Maybe they really could make this work. Before she could say anything, her stomach rumbled loudly. Valentin laughed.

"I guess that's my cue to serve dinner," he said.

"I guess it is," she answered, feeling lighter than she had in a long time.

"Where shall we set up?"

"There's the meeting table over there, or we could just sit on the floor by the coffee table." She gestured toward a long sofa that faced a coffee table and two easy chairs.

"Coffee table it is," he said and moved away.

She watched as he set everything up and fell a little more in love with him as he laid their meal out.

"Dion's hard work?" she asked as she settled beside him on the couch and accepted a glass of red wine.

"You really don't want to try my cooking," he replied with a grimace. "So, yeah, it's Dion to the rescue again."

"Thank goodness for Dion," she murmured. "So, shall we make a toast?"

"To us?"

"To us," she affirmed as they clinked glasses and each took a sip of wine.

"Let me look after you," Valentin said, putting his glass back on the table.

"I certainly won't object to that," she said. "It's been a long day."

"Tell me about it," he encouraged. "You don't often talk about your work."

"You don't often ask," she answered simply.

"I'm sorry about that. I will try harder in the future,

Imogene. I promise. I want to be the husband you deserve."

"You are right now," she said, accepting a plate of steaming spaghetti from him.

"No," he corrected her. "But I will be. Just you wait and see."

She had no answer for that but again, that sense of light and joy filled her inside. Maybe they could make this work after all.

While they dined she let Valentin coax the details of her day from her, and bit by bit she found herself relaxing more and more. When it came to discussing business, he was so easy to talk to, she noted. A shame they'd struggled so much about other things. But that was changing, wasn't it?

Partway through dinner, Valentin had risen and played with her iPod dock, which sat on a credenza behind her desk. He'd chosen an easy listening playlist and once they'd eaten their fill, he put out one hand to her.

"I want to dance with you, Imogene," he said in a voice that brooked no argument.

She smiled her response. They hadn't danced since the stiff formal wedding dance almost three months ago. "I'd like that."

He pulled her to her feet and into his arms and they began to move together, swaying gently to the music, not dancing quite so much as simply being together. It was beautiful, and it lit a familiar slow-burning need deep inside her. But even so, her in-

securities still hovered on the edge of her thoughts. She loved Valentin and she loved being with him, but until he'd fully resolved the situation with Carla she didn't feel as though they could confidently move forward together. But he was taking steps to do that now, she reminded herself as he nuzzled the curve of her neck, sending a shiver of liquid fire to burn through her body. And was it that she didn't trust him, or didn't trust Carla Rogers?

Definitely the latter, she decided. But that didn't mean that Valentin was completely out of the woods in that department. He'd made promises to her tonight, promises that were likely going to be a challenge to keep. The proof would be in what came next, she decided, giving herself over to the man holding her in his arms. The only man who'd ever had the ability to make her blood sing with desire. The only man she'd ever loved.

When Valentin's hands began to move over her back, his fingers playing with the zipper that ran the length of her back, she whispered a soft "Yes" in his ear before biting gently on his earlobe. It was all the encouragement he needed to undo her dress. The sensation of his hot, broad hands on her bare skin was temptation and bliss rolled into one. With the fingers of one hand he unsnapped her bra, then reached up to push the fabric of her dress down off her shoulders, easing her arms out of the long sleeves and letting her bra and dress fall to the floor in a pool around her feet. Her whole body hummed with

need. Need for him to take her, to touch her, to taste her—everywhere.

"Lock my door," she instructed, stepping out of the puddle of fabric.

He did so, quickly, and returned to face her.

"You are so beautiful," Valentin said gently as he looked at her.

His eyes roamed every inch of her exposed skin, his fingers now tracing the edges of her garter belt, then the edges of her panties. She could barely swallow, such was the intensity of the wave of desire that hit her.

"I want you, Valentin," she said on a voice that shook with emotion. "Make love to me."

"Your wish is my absolute command."

He lifted her into his arms and carried her over to the couch they'd only recently vacated, and laid her there before reaching for his clothing and shedding it with an economy of motion that impressed her.

"I never knew you could move so fast," she teased from her recumbent position.

"With the right incentive, I can do anything." He grinned, settling over her.

"Anytime, anywhere?"

"For you, always."

And then he showed her. His hands skimmed her breasts, his touch light as a feather and making her skin prick into goose bumps and her nipples draw into tight beads. Lower and lower he let his fingers drift down her body, unsnapping the catches on her garter belt and, one by one, rolling her stockings

down her legs. As he reached each foot, he massaged the instep, his touch sending wild jolts of pleasure through her. Then he worked his way back up again—his touch sure and strong this time. He gently massaged her calves, her thighs, and then reached to tug her panties down and expose her to him completely. She shivered in anticipation as his hands cupped her buttocks and he bent to flick his tongue against her thigh, then to the curve that indented at the top, before doing the same to the other leg.

"Valentin, you're driving me crazy."

"You want me to stop?"

"No, don't stop. Whatever you do, don't stop." She heard him laugh and lifted her head to look at him. His eyes had darkened to indigo and they shimmered with desire and love and just a sprinkling of mischief. Oh, how she loved this man. Loved how he made her feel, loved what he did to her. "Please, don't stop," she reiterated in a voice that could barely be heard.

Without taking his gaze from hers, he lowered his mouth to her and she gasped as he flicked his tongue against her sensitive bud. "Like this?" he asked.

"Like that," she managed.

"Or maybe more like this?" he asked before closing his mouth around her and sucking gently and rhythmically at her.

Her eyes closed involuntarily, her head fell back on the cushions, as sensation overtook her body and she climbed to the apex of pleasure and then tipped over into the abyss, her body lifting on the waves of

pleasure that threatened to rob her very consciousness. When the pleasure began to slowly seep away, she felt him move again, heard the sound of him opening a condom packet and covering himself. Then she felt the blunt tip of his penis pressing into her swollen slick flesh, felt herself stretch and mold to accommodate him. She lifted legs that felt weak, like jelly, and buried her heels into his buttocks, lifting her hips and letting him slide deeper inside her. She groaned on a new wave of pleasure as he pressed against her.

"And like that," she said on a moan. "Just like that."

Valentin kissed her deeply, his tongue sweeping her mouth as his hips began to move, at first slowly, then more quickly as the momentum of their joining overtook them both.

"I can't hold back," he groaned against his mouth.

"I don't want you to," she replied, her hands tightening on his shoulders as she began to feel her second orgasm build deep inside her. Different from before. Stronger, deeper.

She felt his body surge, then surge again. A cry tore from his throat as his entire body tensed and shook and pulsed with the power of his climax. And as he shuddered against her she went over the edge again, soaring on a physical joy so intense, so incomprehensible in its strength, that she knew she was bonded to Valentin forever.

Fourteen

Tonight they were joining Alice Horvath for dinner. Imogene was a little worried about how it would go. Valentin had been very annoyed at being manipulated by his grandmother into their marriage, but Imogene had to admit, even though she'd been angry at first herself and while they'd had a rocky time of it, they were working things out. It was something they'd never have done on their own. And the longer Imogene was with Valentin, the more she knew he was the only man for her. She only wished she could be 100 percent certain he felt the same way.

He said and did all the right things—she knew he'd had meetings with his legal team and Human Resources regarding the situation with Carla—but

as far as she knew, the woman was still very firmly entrenched in his day-to-day life. And after that stunt when Carla had come to Imogene's office, Imogene didn't trust her one little bit. With a sigh of resignation, she turned away from the walk-in closet, two dresses in her hands.

"Which one?" she asked Valentin, holding them both up for his perusal.

One was the purple dress she'd worn to his office the night they'd made love there, the other, something new she'd spied on a rare shopping trip with her mother the other day. Valentin nodded toward the new dress.

"That greeny-colored one. I like what it does to your eyes."

She laughed. "You haven't seen it on, so how do you know what it does to my eyes?"

"Trust me, I'm a man. I know these things," he said calmly before kissing her firmly on the lips. "By the way, I wanted to tell you that we had a meeting at work today. My legal team and a representative from HR and me, together with Carla and her legal representative. She has accepted a very healthy severance package and will be leaving Horvath Pharmaceuticals immediately. I thought you would want to know that everything's been taken care of."

Emotion threatened to overwhelm her. He'd done it. For her. For them. "Oh, Valentin, I don't know what to say."

"'Thank you' will suffice. And maybe a kiss to em-
bellish your thanks?" he suggested with a wry smile.

She did both, tossing both dresses on the bed and
rushing across the room to jump at him.

"Thank you," she said again as they drew apart.

"I'm sorry it took me so long. Maybe now we can
carry on with a clean slate, yes?"

"Yes, I'd like that," Imogene replied vehemently.

"Good, then let's finish getting ready. If there's
one thing my grandmother can't stand it's a lack of
punctuality."

He went through to the bathroom and Imogene
recovered her dresses from the bed, holding each
one in front of her in turn, as she stood opposite the
full-length mirror. He was right, she realized. The
teal gown did make her eyes sparkle and glow. Or
maybe it was just him, she thought as she hung the
purple dress back in the closet. It had been two weeks
since that night he'd come to her office. Two weeks
of the kind of marriage she'd always wanted with
him. Two weeks filled with hope and love and plans
for a future she'd begun to think she'd never achieve.
And now she knew her hope hadn't been misplaced.
Without the shadow of Carla in their lives, she knew
they would make it.

When they got to the restaurant at the Waldorf,
Alice was already seated at their table. As they approached, she rose from her chair, offering her cheek
first to her grandson and then to Imogene.

"You two look happy," she said with a genuine smile.

"We are," Imogene said as Valentin helped his grandmother to be seated again. "But it remains a work in progress."

"Marriage is always a work in progress. It never stops being one, nor should it," Alice said sagely before focusing her attention on Valentin. "You look better, my boy. Less strained."

"Thank you, Nagy. And you look as beautiful as ever."

His grandmother blushed at the compliment but Imogene noticed Alice wasn't looking quite as well as she had nearly three months ago.

They turned their conversation to more general things, Valentin's brother, Galen, included.

"He's coping better with fatherhood than I expected," Alice admitted after taking a sip of the champagne she'd ordered for the table. "Ellie is a charming child. Missing her parents, obviously, but she loves Galen. She has a fear, though, that he'll be taken from her unexpectedly, like her parents were."

"Understandable, I suppose," Valentin said. "No one could have predicted her losing both of them like that."

"Yes, but Galen's taking it seriously. He's asked me to find him a wife. One who wants a ready-made family."

Imogene looked as her husband sat back and stared at his grandmother in shock. "A wife? Oh,

no, not Galen. Not through Match Made in Marriage anyway."

"And why not?" Alice bristled visibly, bright spots of color rising to her cheeks.

"Not for Galen. Not with everything else he's dealing with. You have to admit, both your pairings for family members didn't start out so well."

Imogene knew he was referring to his cousin Ilya's rocky start to marriage with his business rival Yasmin Carter. Yasmin had left her husband early on in the marriage, but they'd worked things out in the end and had appeared to be very much in love at her and Valentin's ceremony. But she knew Valentin had a point and she watched as Alice's expression set in stone, much as it probably did back in the days when she ran the entire Horvath Corporation—an iron hand in a velvet glove, she'd heard it described as—and no one had dared go against her.

Alice looked at her grandson. "Are you saying the two of you are in crisis?"

She watched as Valentin and Imogene exchanged a glance.

"It hasn't been smooth sailing."

She sniffed audibly. "As I said before, marriage is a constant work in progress. Are you two giving up?"

"No, definitely not," Valentin hastened to assure her.

"Then why should Galen not find his perfect match?" she pressed, irritated beyond belief that

Valentin had the gall to suggest she not find Galen's future bride.

The all-too-familiar pain in her chest asserted itself again. She didn't have time for this now, she thought angrily, and she was equally annoyed that this dinner, which was supposed to be a happy celebration, had started on the wrong foot.

"I just don't think Match Made in Marriage is the right vehicle for Galen to find long-term happiness," Valentin said, sticking to his guns as he always had, even as a child.

"Well, it's a good thing he feels differently. I'm already screening our database for a suitable applicant. Now," she said, indicating an end to the subject, "let's concentrate on the purpose of this evening."

"And that is?" Valentin asked with one of his disdainful looks down his perfectly straight nose.

A nose that had looked equally handsome on the dear face of her late husband, Eduard. It was moments like this, when she caught glimpses of her late husband in the wonderfully large and growing family they'd created, that she missed him so very, very much. The niggle in her chest grew a little tighter.

"To celebrate your impending three-month milestone, of course. Unless you've come here tonight to tell me you're separating at that juncture?"

She gave them both her most supercilious stare, daring them to refute the evidence she'd seen with her own eyes as they'd entered the restaurant together. She'd observed the solicitous way Valen-

tin had taken his wife's coat. Watched as his hand had lingered on her shoulder and how Imogene had smiled at him, her eyes never leaving his for a moment. This was not a couple on the verge of separating.

"Of course not, Mrs. Horvath," Imogene hastened to assure her.

"Imogene, call me Alice or Nagy. We're family now," she instructed her granddaughter-in-law with a benevolent smile. "So, we're celebrating, yes?"

To her great relief, the two of them exchanged another of their deep and meaningful glances, then both nodded. The sensation in her chest eased a little, allowing her to draw in a deeper breath.

"Good," she said. "Then I propose a toast. To Imogene and Valentin and their long and happy and, dare I say it, fruitful marriage."

"Well, isn't all this just darling?"

Alice stopped midsip as another woman came to stand by their table. She looked up at the petite creature. Pretty enough, but with a hardness about her face that was distinctly off-putting. And there was something else about her, an energy that bordered on frenzy. Whatever it was, it made her feel very uncomfortable. Alice glanced across the table to see whether Valentin or Imogene had any inkling as to who the creature was. Imogene's features had frozen into a mask of disbelief while Valentin looked angrier than she'd ever seen him.

"I'm sorry," Alice said, when the others failed to

speak. "You have me at a disadvantage. I'm Alice Horvath, and you are?"

"Carla Rogers," the other woman said. "Ask Valentin, he knows me. Well."

"Carla, please leave. This is a private family function," Valentin said sternly. "We said all we needed to say in the meeting today."

"You may have. However, there is one little detail I think your wife ought to know," Carla said firmly. Then, placing the palm of one hand over her lower belly, she looked at Imogene. "Please, do the right thing. His child deserves to know its father, not be banished into oblivion."

The pain in Alice's chest increased tenfold as the dreadful woman's words sank in. Valentin's child? With this creature?

Imogene rose abruptly to her feet, her chair toppling behind her as she did so. "No," she said in a voice that shook with horror and emotion. She turned to Valentin, who looked equally shocked. "She's pregnant? With your baby? So this is how you *take care of things*? I believed you when you said it was over. I *won't* stand for this. It's the final straw. I can't stay in a marriage riddled with lies!"

"She's the one lying, Imogene. I told you the truth." Valentin rose also and reached for his wife, but she was already moving out of range.

Alice stood, too, her legs unsteady and her breathing becoming more and more difficult as the pressure in her chest built.

"Imogene, please, wait." Alice caught Imogene's arm as she made to brush past, halting her in her tracks. She then directed her attention to the interloper. "And you, Ms. Rogers, leave us this instant. You're not welcome here."

That was all she managed before the pain became overwhelming. She could no longer draw a breath and the faces in front of her began to swim and blur before disappearing altogether as she collapsed slowly to the restaurant floor.

Imogene did her best to catch Alice as she crumpled, but caught unawares, she could do little but break her fall. She looked back as she heard Valentin cry out, "Nagy!"

He moved quickly to his grandmother's side. Imogene remained rooted where she was, recognizing instantly that her husband's beloved grandmother was possibly dying of a heart attack before his very eyes. Valentin looked up at Carla, who stood to one side, staring at the tableau before her with a strangely blank expression on her face.

"Carla, I need your assistance. I'll do compressions and you breathe for her," he said abruptly.

Without looking to see if Carla had followed his directive, he straightened Alice on the restaurant floor, checking her vital signs as he did so. Then he began compressions, at the same time looking up for Carla. It was only logical that he would, Imogene told herself. Carla was a doctor after all. They'd worked

together in the ER in Africa. They were experienced with this high-need urgent-action situation. But Carla turned her back on them all and started toward the door. Imogene moved to intercept her.

"Help him," she urged. "He needs you."

"He doesn't need me. He chose you," she said bitterly and continued walking.

"You're a doctor. You can't just walk away!" Imogene cried out to Carla's retreating back.

Carla looked over her shoulder. "Watch me," she said coldly and continued for the door.

Imogene looked back at Valentin, who kept up compressions on Alice's tiny frail chest, keeping her heart beating for her when it had given up on itself. There was no time for hesitation. She pushed through the growing crowd that had formed around them and knelt on the floor opposite Valentin.

"I've done CPR training, but only ever on a dummy," she said with a faint tremor in her voice. "Tell me exactly what you need me to do."

Without breaking his rhythm on his grandmother's chest, he gave Imogene clear instructions.

"Where's Carla? I asked for her help," he said, briefly looking up and around to see where she was.

"I saw her walk out the restaurant soon after Alice collapsed," Imogene said between breaths. "It doesn't matter. You don't need her here."

Imogene forced back the instinctive sense of being second choice in her husband's life. The woman

might be carrying his baby, but she wasn't here for him when he needed her most.

They worked in tandem until a commotion behind them announced the arrival of an emergency team. Valentin gave the details to the lead paramedic and only sat back as the highly trained EMTs, armed with a defibrillator, took over. He didn't relax until he heard the magic words. "We've got a pulse."

Imogene went to Valentin's side. Despite everything, she still wanted to comfort him. "She's going to be okay, Valentin."

"I can't lose her. Not because of this," he said brokenly as the paramedics began transferring Alice to a gurney.

"You won't. Go now. Go with her."

Even though the paramedics were beginning to wheel Alice away, he hesitated, his hands grasping Imogene's. He looked feverishly into her eyes. "Imogene, Carla was lying. She's not carrying my baby. It's impossible. I promise you."

"It's not important now."

"It is important that you believe me. Please, say you'll wait for me, that you won't do anything rash until we've spoken properly."

"I won't go anywhere. Not yet."

"Sir, are you coming with us in the ambulance?" one of the emergency team asked.

"Yes, I'm a doctor. I'll travel with my grandmother." He turned back to Imogene one more time. "Please, wait for me," he pleaded before pressing an

urgent kiss against her lips and then moving quickly through the restaurant to follow the gurney.

Imogene stood there, oblivious to the people milling around her asking her if she was okay. She finally sat down in a vacant chair at what had been their table and began to shake as the reality of what had just happened sank in. Carla's arrival. Her bald statement. Alice's heart attack. Working with Valentin to save her life. It was all too much.

"Ma'am, can we assist you with a ride home?" the restaurant manager asked. "Or perhaps to the hospital?"

"I…I'm not sure where they're taking her, to be honest. But, yes, our driver can be reached at this number."

She fumbled in her bag for a card and gave it to the manager.

"Perhaps you'd like to wait downstairs in the hotel lobby? It will be a little more private for you than here, I suspect," he suggested. "I can arrange for someone to sit with you until your car arrives."

"That won't be necessary. Just the car, please."

Imogene nodded her thanks and rose to her feet to follow him. While he called for her driver, she retrieved her coat from the coat check, then headed down to the lobby. Suddenly desperate for the cool fresh night air and to get away from the heat and chatter that had surrounded her inside, Imogene went out through the front doors of the hotel. A movement

in the shadows to one side startled her and she stifled a groan of disbelief as Carla materialized beside her.

"Haven't you done enough damage?" she growled at the other woman.

"You're one to talk. Your marriage is nothing but a sham. Valentin loves me. Always has and always will. We'd still be together if you hadn't come along again and distracted him. You have no idea how hard I've worked to get him back. How patient I've been."

"Perhaps the fact that you had to work so hard at it was an indication that your feelings for him weren't reciprocated?"

"It doesn't matter what you say. He loves me. I know he does. And now with the baby, I think it's time you step aside and leave him, this time for good."

Imogene looked at Carla and was shocked at the unnatural brightness in her eyes. Her words were those of a madwoman, not the calm, cool, collected doctor she'd met in Africa and certainly not the intelligent and gifted head of research and development that she'd heard Carla described as. Perhaps losing her position at Horvath Pharmaceuticals had unhinged her completely.

But no matter how she felt about her, the woman was pregnant and out here in the cold night without a coat and, judging by the way she was hanging around, without a ride home. Clearly she needed help. Pushing aside her own feelings of anger and

betrayal toward her husband and her definite dislike and distrust of Carla, Imogene made an offer.

"I can get you help, Carla. I really think you need it. But first of all, let me see you home."

"Why?" Carla retorted, looking at Imogene as if she were the one who'd gone completely crazy. "I've slept with your husband. I'm doing my best to break up your marriage again. Why would you be nice to me?"

Imogene looked at Carla and spoke quietly and steadily, seeing her car draw near. "Because you need help and because," she said as an alternate spin on the situation began to bloom in her mind, "I'm not entirely sure I believe you right now. Look, let me give you a ride home."

To her shock Carla dissolved into tears. The doorman looked at the two women with concern and began to walk toward them, but Imogene gestured for him to stay back.

"Come on, Carla. My driver is here. Let's go."

Wrapping one arm around the other woman's waist, she guided her into the back seat of the car.

"A slight detour today, Anton. We'll be seeing Ms. Rogers home first."

"And Mr. Horvath?"

"There's been an incident with his grandmother. He's gone to the hospital with her."

Anton expressed his regrets before steering the car into traffic.

"Carla, give Anton your address."

"It's all right, Mrs. Horvath. I already know it," Anton replied smoothly before Carla could answer.

Imogene's body felt as though it had been cast in stone. She could barely breathe as the ramifications and possibilities of that one statement surged through her. Did that mean that Valentin was frequently driven to Carla's home? That every word from his mouth had been a lie? That he wouldn't, or couldn't, let Carla go from his life? That he was just like her father after all?

She tried to swallow against the lump that threatened to block her throat and felt her eyes burn with unshed tears. She'd be damned before she'd cry in front of this woman. No matter that she'd chosen to help her, there was no way she would show weakness in front of her, too.

On the other side of the back seat, Carla sat huddled against her door. Her crying had slowed to an occasional sob, and in the dark interior she eventually lifted her head and looked at Imogene.

"I'm sorry," she said brokenly.

"Are you?" Imogene tried to keep her voice neutral. Not easy given the shock she'd just received. "What for, precisely?"

"All of it. Africa. Here. Tonight."

Imogene held her silence, hoping it might prompt Carla to continue. Even in the dark she could see what a mess Carla had been reduced to after her crying jag. Imogene reached into her bag for a small pack of tissues and silently handed them across.

Carla accepted them with a small thank-you. After a few more minutes, she finished mopping her face and blowing her nose and straightened in her seat.

"I'm not pregnant," she said bluntly.

A massive wave of relief flooded through every inch of Imogene's body. She'd begun to suspect that Carla had been staging it all in a last-ditch effort to drive her away. Not trusting herself to speak, she held her silence. Besides, there was still the issue of Valentin's visits to Carla's home to be worked out.

"And I lied about Valentin being my lover that day in Africa. He was still at work. I'd brought one of the new doctors back to your house with me. I knew you'd likely show up at some point and I wanted to use that to my advantage."

"What do you expect me to say?" Imogene blurted out, anger beginning to boil just beneath the surface.

Carla had manipulated them all—Imogene, Valentin and her poor unsuspecting lover, who'd been showering when Imogene had arrived home that day.

"I don't know. I hope that one day you might be able to forgive me."

"I don't know if I can do that," Imogene said through lips that felt frozen and immobile.

All those years wasted. All that unhappiness. All for a lie.

"I understand. I wouldn't if the situation was reversed." She shifted in her seat and plucked at the seat belt that crossed her body with a listless hand. "Valentin was the only man to ever end a relation-

ship with me. It only made me want him all the more. Of course there have been others since him, but no one has ever matched Valentin. He was always my end goal."

"You speak about him as if he had no choice in the matter. As if he were something to acquire, not a flesh and blood man to love and care for."

Carla looked away from Imogene and out the window. "You love him, don't you?" Without waiting for an answer, she continued, "He never stopped loving you, you know. Through all these years he's constantly rebuffed my attentions, and those of anyone else who dared make an advance on him. You were always the only one for him. It drove me crazy. I'm not very gracious in loss, as you've probably gathered. I hope you'll believe me when I say I am truly sorry, to you both."

Imogene let Carla's words wash over her and slowly penetrate the frozen shell that had locked her in place. Slowly she became aware that Anton had pulled up to the curb in front of an apartment building in Greenwich Village.

"I won't trouble you again," Carla said. "Thanks for the ride home."

Before Imogene could say another word, Carla had let herself out and was walking toward the entrance. Once she was gone from view, Imogene met Anton's gaze in the rearview mirror.

"Do you think she'll be all right?" she asked.

"She's a tough one. She'll get through it," he said.

"And, since I couldn't help overhearing—I just want to clear something up for you. Mr. Horvath never accompanied Ms. Rogers to her apartment."

"I know that," Imogene conceded.

Now all she had to do was work this out with her husband.

Fifteen

Imogene entered their apartment and was struck by its emptiness. Every night these past few weeks Valentin had greeted her on her arrival home. Now, of course, he was at the hospital, no doubt worried sick about Alice. She checked her phone to see if he'd messaged or called her yet. Nothing. At least that had to be good news, right? she told herself as she shrugged out of her coat and hung it in the closet off the foyer. Her stomach rumbled. They hadn't even had the chance to place an order tonight, let alone eat anything. But even though she was hungry, she didn't know if she could stomach anything right now.

She wandered to their bedroom and kicked off her shoes, sitting on the bed for a while and pondering

what she should do. She felt restless, her mind still in turmoil over Carla's sudden about-face and her apologies. It made Imogene want to turn it all over in her mind again. To examine every step of her journey with Valentin and to see where she allowed herself to be so badly duped.

Had it all been Carla's manipulation, or had she been an easy victim because of her own preconceptions? She admitted she'd gone into her whirlwind relationship with Valentin starry-eyed but holding back a piece of herself all the way. Yes, she'd been wooed by Valentin's attentions, had fallen hard and fast in love. But had she given him her all? If she had, would she have felt more secure?

She got up from the bed and walked through the apartment to the bedroom that had been converted into a den for their private use. Cozier than the formal lounge and perhaps a little more inviting than the library, it contained comfortable furniture and shelves filled with knickknacks and books, as well as Valentin's enviable movie collection. Entering the room, Imogene made a beeline for the shelves that housed Valentin's old photo albums. She'd teased him about them, telling him he was archaic because didn't everyone store everything digitally these days? But he'd remained staunch in his old-school values and reiterated to her the pleasure he found in thumbing through the albums, reliving highlights of the past.

She knew exactly which one she wanted and slid

it from the stack. The date on the spine was seven years ago, the title, quite simply, *Africa*.

Opening the album to the beginning, she was instantly cast back to the central African nation where they'd been volunteering—to the heat, the smells, the sounds, the people. Her contract had only been supposed to be a short one, filling in for another teacher who had been called home to an emergency. But she'd talked of extending her stay to tie in with the completion of Valentin's contract. Until Carla.

Imogene's eyes blurred and she blinked away the unexpected moisture before turning the page. She felt a jolt of shock as she studied the photos there and her gaze locked on a younger, happier version of herself, caught midlaugh by Valentin's lens as she attempted to drink from a gourd for the first—and last—time. The expression in her eyes as she stared into the lens struck her, reminding her of how very much she'd loved him then.

But it was nothing compared to how she felt about him now. Her emotions were so much deeper. Stronger, even. Shrouded, yes, with the fear of being hurt again, but deeper nonetheless. She stared at the younger version of herself and then turned the page, this time to a photo of the two of them, oblivious to the person taking the shot, with eyes only for each other. He'd been her first real love and, she realized, he was her only real love, too. Now or ever. But had she ever really told him that? Shown him?

No, she'd never allowed herself to love him as fully as he deserved.

Her entire first marriage with Valentin had been based on her waiting and watching for him to show signs of her father's behavior. Of him disengaging from her and pursuing other women while maintaining the facade of a happy union. She'd basically handed him to Carla on a platter, she realized in retrospect. She'd gone through the motions of being his wife, of trusting him and loving him, but she'd never really trusted him at all. Instead she'd been waiting for him to show he had feet of clay, unable to believe that he could love her as she so desperately wanted to be loved. Waiting for him to be the man her father was. Charming, yes. Dedicated to his work, definitely. Dedicated to his family? Well, when it suited. She hadn't wanted that, and by making that her focus, that was exactly what she'd ended up with.

Instead of looking for the differences between Valentin and her father, she'd looked only for the similarities and where she'd found them, they'd derailed her confidence, derailed her conviction that their love was forever and that their marriage was a perfect match.

Imogene turned the pages on the album more swiftly now, noticed the changes in herself—her expression, her posture. She could track the outgoing nature she'd exhibited in the early days of their relationship slowly being snuffed out by her own paranoia about having married a man like her dad.

She gently closed the album and filed it back in the stack, certain now of what she needed to do. It was time to be there for Valentin at the hospital, as a wife ought to be, comforting him through the worry he must be feeling about his grandmother. And then, when he was ready, to tell Valentin the truth about her love for him.

Valentin slumped in the uncomfortable chair in the waiting area while a cardiac team worked hard to stabilize his grandmother behind the curtains in the ER. Every harsh word he'd ever said to her came back to haunt him, making him wish them all unsaid. No matter how angry he'd been at her three months ago, she had his best interests at heart. He should have given her more credit. The problems he and Imogene faced were of their own making, not Nagy's, and it was up to them to make them right again.

If Imogene would still consider it after tonight's debacle, he thought ruefully.

He knew Carla had been lying but he'd never forget the look of raw pain and unadulterated shock that had ripped across Imogene's face, exposing her vulnerability for all to see. He hated that she'd had to be hurt like that again, and by a woman he'd been deaf, dumb and blind about for far too long. But most of all, he hated that even with the rebuilding they'd been doing in the past fortnight, hell, the past three months, she'd believed Carla's lies in an instant.

It wasn't so impossible, he rationalized. Her father

was a class A jerk when it came to marriage, and if that was the best example she'd ever had before her, it was no wonder that she'd believed Carla's lies. Which meant if this was to work between them, he had to work harder.

He closed his eyes and tipped his head back against the wall, frustration making his body tense. He wished he could be on the other side of that curtain, helping the specialists with his grandmother. Be there for her, if nothing else. Not for the first time, he missed being actively involved in medicine. No matter how good and how meaningful the work he was doing now, he would never quite get over the rush of being hands-on in critical situations. Of saving lives. Of making a difference. But that lifestyle had taken its own toll. On him and on his marriage. He hadn't been able to see the cracks forming until it was too late. And once the damage was done, things were too far gone.

And now? Was it too late? Would Imogene ever let him back into her heart, her life?

The gentle touch of a soft hand on his and a hint of the fragrance Imogene always wore swam through the myriad smells around him and made his eyes fly open.

"Valentin, is she okay?"

"I don't know yet," he said, putting his other hand on top of hers as if by doing so he could stop her from pulling away from him again.

She was here, beside him, and he was determined to anchor her to him and not let her get away if he

had anything to do about it. Time ticked past ever so slowly and they sat together with so many unspoken words between them. He took strength from her presence, from the fact that she'd come here, to him. And that she stayed, physically connected and assuring him of her nearness. He would never take her for granted again like he had seven years ago. Back then he'd expected everything to simply flow in a natural current of life. But he hadn't taken into account the rocks and boulders and changes in direction that life and other people could throw at a relationship.

He knew why he'd been so darn naive about marriage. As a child prodigy, his life focus had been on learning, on being the best. And once he'd conquered one educational mountain, he'd tackled another. When his peers and cousins had been attending high school dances and dating, he'd been in premed. When they started college, he was already an intern and dealing with the disbelief and distrust of the patients on the wards when they realized how young he was. So he'd worked harder, longer hours, with everything he had in him. And that was how he'd coped when the link between him and Imogene had begun to falter. When she'd made accusations he'd believed were baseless. When she'd had enough and had her lawyer draw up the papers to dissolve their marriage—signing them and sending them to him for his signature even as she boarded the plane to return to the States.

He felt her fingers tighten around his hand.

"Valentin? They're asking for you," she said.

Fear gripped him.

"Dr. Horvath?"

"Yes," he said, rising to his feet.

"We've managed to stabilize your grandmother and we'll be moving her up to the ICU now. We'll run more tests in the morning, but she will need surgery, sooner rather than later. We'll discuss that with her in the morning and hope to schedule her in for surgery later tomorrow if we can. I'm sure you understand the need to act quickly."

"Yes, I do. Thank you. Can I see her now?"

"Briefly. Understandably, she's very tired."

He was torn: afraid to abandon Imogene in case she left while he was gone, but fearful that if he didn't see Nagy now, his last memory of her would be of her being wheeled away from him when they'd arrived here at the hospital.

"Go," Imogene urged him. "I'll be waiting right here for you."

He wanted to kiss her but with all the drama of what happened at the restaurant still unresolved between them, he didn't know how well it would be received.

"Dr. Horvath?" the other doctor prompted.

"Yes, I'm coming now."

With one last glance at Imogene, who nodded at him encouragingly, he followed the doctor behind the curtains. As a trauma surgeon, seeing a patient hooked up to monitors and having tubes running in

and out of their body had been an everyday thing for him. Seeing his grandmother like that was quite another matter. He felt as if he'd abandoned all his medical experience on the other side of the curtain, leaving just the anxious grandson here in the cubicle with her. He hastened forward and took her hand, automatically checking the pulse at her wrist. Not as strong and steady as it should be, but there. He looked down on his grandmother's wrinkled face and felt her mortality hit him square in the chest. They had to do everything to make her well again.

She'd persevered through so much—fleeing Hungary with her parents before the outbreak of World War II, settling into a new and foreign life in the States. Supporting her husband, Eduard, through the establishment of Horvath Aviation and subsequently expanding into the Horvath Corporation. Losing her beloved husband too early to a heart attack. Then losing two of her sons to the same congenital affliction soon after—his own father one of them. Through it all she'd done everything she could to hold her family together. And her family had a lot to be grateful for. They'd rally around to support her now that she needed them most. If she could just hang on.

Her eyes flickered open. "Valentin?"

"You're in the hospital, Nagy. You've had a heart attack."

"Stupid heart pills didn't work," she grumbled behind her oxygen mask.

Heart pills? He wondered how long she'd been

taking medication and if anyone in the family knew. Likely not, he reasoned. Nagy was nothing if not fiercely proud and independent. A trait he'd exhibited himself a time or two.

"We'll get you better, don't worry."

"Imogene?" There was a querulous note to her voice that concerned him. The last thing she needed now was any anxiety.

"She's outside, waiting. Don't worry. We'll sort everything out."

"Something I needed to tell you both," she said weakly. "Important."

Behind him he heard the arrival of the orderlies, ready to take her up to the ICU. "Later, Nagy. They need to get you settled on the ward now. We'll talk later, okay? I promise."

Her eyes slid closed and he stepped aside as the team gathered around his grandmother, attaching and reattaching monitors, before moving her out the cubicle and down the hall to the elevator.

"Excuse me, sir," a nurse said as she bustled into the area. "We need to set up for our next patient."

"Certainly, sorry," he said and walked back toward the waiting area—to Imogene.

Would she still be there? He didn't realize how tense he was until he saw her beautiful but pale face turn toward him. She rose and walked to meet him halfway. A symbol of their future? He hoped so with every cell in his body.

Sixteen

When they returned to the apartment, Imogene felt as if she'd been away from it for days, not merely a few hours. And if she felt that way, how did Valentin feel? she wondered.

"Can I get you something?" she said, moving toward the kitchen. "Dion's bound to have some magical creation in the fridge if you're hungry."

"Maybe a sandwich," he said, following her. "I'll help."

Despite their familiarity with each other and despite their proximity in the kitchen, Imogene couldn't help feeling there was a massive gulf yawning between them. They needed to talk. She needed to tell him she was ready to accept a great deal of the blame

that had led to their initial separation, not to mention the difficulties they'd faced since.

"Shall we take these through to the den?" she suggested as she cut the bread diagonally in halves.

"Good idea," Valentin replied, picking up the tray with the plates on them and carrying it through.

They settled side by side on the massive sofa, each reaching for a sandwich and chewing in a continued awkward silence.

"So, they're—"

"Imogene, I—"

They both started simultaneously, then laughed awkwardly.

"You first," he said.

"I just wanted to ask about Alice. They're doing surgery tomorrow?"

"She'll have an angiography first, I imagine, to confirm their suspicions. Then surgery."

"She's strong, Valentin. She'll pull through."

"A lot of that will depend on the damage to her heart muscle but, yeah, she's strong. Which reminds me. Before we talk, and I mean really talk, I need to let the family know what's happened."

"Of course," Imogene said.

She watched as he scrolled through his phone, calling his eldest cousin, Ilya, first, then his brother, Galen. The other men agreed to let the rest of the family, mostly based on the West Coast, know about their matriarch. Valentin slid his phone onto the coffee table and leaned back on the sofa.

"Well, that went more easily than I anticipated."

"It's good that they're all there for you. Families should always be like that."

"Yes, but you didn't have that growing up, did you?" Valentin said, obviously seizing the opportunity to turn the conversation toward the subject they'd both been so carefully stepping around.

"No, I didn't. I admit, I didn't realize until tonight exactly how much that altered my perception of everything. Of everyone. Including you."

"Do you want to explain?" he prompted.

She pulled one leg up underneath her and turned to face him on the sofa. "I *need* to explain it to you. You've seen what my family is like. Isolated satellites, orbiting around each other. Occasionally living the same life in the same room, but that's no life at all. Not for me, at least. If I were more like them, maybe I could handle that. But—"

"But you're not like that at all," Valentin interrupted. "You have too much heart. And I was too stupid to see that. Imogene, you have to believe me, I haven't been conducting an affair with Carla under your nose or while we were apart. I didn't do it in Africa. I didn't do it here. In fact, since you, there's been no one else—which has been mighty uncomfortable at times," he said with an attempt at humor.

Imogene looked at him and knew he was telling her the truth. This proud, intense, focused man had more honor in his little finger than her father had

in his entire body. Why had she been so reluctant to see that?

"Same," she said softly. "I couldn't bear the thought of someone else touching me, being with me. I knew I'd have to get over it eventually. I was prepared to push myself. I thought if I entered into a Match Made in Marriage I'd be paired with someone so compatible that the sexual side of the marriage would be a natural progression."

"And it was," he commented wryly.

"Yes, it was. It *is*," she affirmed. "I know you weren't unfaithful to me. I'm sorry I ever thought that you were capable of being so cruel and cavalier about the vows we made to each other. It's easy to blame my parents but the fault lies with me. Rather than see the truth before my eyes, I went looking for trouble. Carla, it seems, was only too happy to provide it."

"I wish I'd listened to you then. Properly listened. Understood how she made you feel."

"How I allowed myself to feel," Imogene corrected. "I need to own up to this. To take my life and my feelings and reactions back under my control. I gave her power over me back in Africa. And she made the most of it. Did you know you're the only man ever to refuse her? That's part of why she wanted you so badly."

"We went out briefly, but like I said to you a long time ago, it burned out quickly. At least it did for me. I didn't understand it, but she obviously never took my breaking things off with any finality, more as an abeyance—something to be resumed later."

Imogene nodded in understanding. "I couldn't believe it when she turned up tonight, especially after what you'd told me here at home. But I'm so sorry I believed her when she said she was pregnant with your baby. I just—" Her voice broke off and it took her a few moments to get her emotions under control. "I just felt so betrayed. I want children—our children— so very much, and to have her stand there and baldly announce she was having your baby? It just cut me in two. I would never stand in the way of anyone and their child the way my father's mistresses have with me. I would have left you for that reason alone, so you could create a family with her and your baby."

Imogene's voice had grown thicker with every word until she was beyond speech. Tears began to roll down her cheeks and she swiped them away angrily. She didn't want to be the kind of woman who used tears as a weapon or to manipulate a situation. She needed to be strong, for herself and for Valentin. Her distrust of him was a serious issue. One she needed to overcome. If she couldn't, then what hope did they have?

"And that's a part of what makes you so special, Genie," Valentin said, moving closer and pulling her into his arms. "It's one of the reasons I love you so much. You're my everything. Did you know that? Since the day I met you, you've never been far from my thoughts. I admit I wasn't the best husband the first time around, and I'm probably not doing such a great job this time around, either. I've needed to

learn to put you first, before my work. It hasn't been easy but I know we can do it. We can make our life together a rich one and we can build that family we both want together.

"Tonight consolidated that for me. When Nagy collapsed at the restaurant I was terrified that I was going to lose her. How on earth would I be able to explain that to my family? Me, a doctor, unable to do anything to save my own grandmother? I guess what they say about having a God complex is kind of true. So many times I've held people's lives, literally, in my hands. But I've never been frightened about my ability to do what I've been trained to do until tonight, and going through that reminded me of how I felt when you left me. I didn't know what to do. Logic should have told me to follow you home, to fight for you, but I did the only thing I knew I could be a success at—work. So I signed another contract, stayed in Africa another year, and when I got home I threw myself into Horvath Pharmaceuticals, doing everything I could to forget you. To forget my failure with you. But I failed at that as much as I had failed you in our marriage. I couldn't forget you and I found I didn't want to."

He took in a deep breath before continuing. "Yes, I was angry when I saw that Nagy had paired us up at Port Ludlow. But most of all I was angry with myself because I had failed where she had succeeded. Despite how I felt about you, I never reached out to you, I never visited you here at home even though I

knew you were most likely still here in New York. I made no effort and for that I am truly, deeply sorry. I wouldn't blame you if you wanted to leave me now.

"Imogene, know this—I love you and I want you to be happy, but if you can't bring yourself to trust me I know you'll never be happy in our marriage. I know what love is now. And I know that I'm prepared to let you walk away from me again, rather than hold you to vows that neither of us were probably ready to make in the first place. I should have put you first then, too. Should have let you walk away from Nagy and her pressure on us, if that's what you wanted. Instead, seeing you again reminded me all too viscerally of how much I still wanted you. I was prepared to do anything to persuade you to give us another chance, but I did that without considering what it would do to you if we failed again."

"Valentin, I agreed to go ahead with our marriage. It was a mutual decision that day. Yes, my initial instinct was to run like hell in the opposite direction, but when push came to shove, I couldn't do it. The moment I saw you, my body recognized you and was drawn to you. It's always been that way between us, but that's worked to our detriment, too."

Valentin buried his face in her hair and inhaled the scent that always served to calm and incite him at the same time. It was that very juxtaposition that lay at the base of their union. Could they manage to work through that? Could they honestly make this

a solid, tangible thing and move forward stronger than before? Or would they implode all over again?

"If you choose to stay with me, Imogene, I want you to know it's forever this time. I won't let you go again and I will spend the rest of my life proving that to you. If you can only love me in return and trust me to cherish and protect that love, I will ensure you never regret your decision for a moment. But if you can't forgive me for the mistakes I've made in the past, for not listening to you, especially when it came to Carla, I will understand. I never really knew what love meant, aside from the family sense or from the physical side of things the first time we married. Not until I lost you. I don't want to lose you again."

Imogene shifted until she was facing Valentin. She could see the worry in his eyes that tonight's episode had pushed her away—had exposed a yawning chasm in their relationship. And she could see his fear that they had no coming back after that. Her heart ached for all the unsaid words between them. For all the love she'd borne for him all these years but never been able to adequately express. She looked him deeply in the eyes.

"Leaving you was a dreadful mistake, I know that now, but not believing you was far, far worse. I am so desperately sorry that I didn't trust you. Carla delivered a few truths to me tonight. She said she had deliberately tried to break us up. I guess she thought that if she couldn't have you, then no one

should, especially not me. I think seeing us together again drove her over the edge. She told me you hadn't touched her from the day you met me. And I find myself wondering why I can believe her, when she spilled her lies or when she admitted them like she did tonight, and not you. It's a flaw in my character that I didn't believe you, not a flaw in yours. Can you forgive me for being so distrustful? For allowing my own experience with my family to create the blueprint for our life together? I have so much to unlearn, but I really want to succeed with you. I love you, Valentin Horvath, with all my heart, but is my love going to be enough?"

"Enough? You love me—that's all I need," Valentin replied.

He cupped her cheeks with his warm hands and kissed her. Not a kiss of passion or of need, but one of affirmation, of promise. Deep in her heart, Imogene began to feel hope for the two of them. When he released her, she chose her words carefully.

"So, you think we can take a chance on each other again? Get it right this time?"

His blue eyes never left hers as he took both her hands in his and kissed each one as if making a vow. His voice, when he spoke, was firm and unequivocal. "Yes."

Imogene clasped his hands tight and got to her feet, pulling him up with her. She led him to the bedroom. *Their* bedroom, she corrected herself. There would be no more his and hers if they were

to make a success of this. There would only be what was theirs. In the semidarkness of their room, she reached for his clothes and began to undress him. Her hands made swift work of the tie at his throat, the buttons of his shirt, the belt at his waist. As she bared more of his skin, she allowed herself the simple pleasure of touching him, with her hands, with her lips, with her tongue. Imprinting the memory of his body indelibly onto her mind and into her heart. When he was naked, she pushed him toward the bed and swiftly stripped off her clothing and followed him onto the mattress.

"I love you, Valentin," she repeated. "I never want to lose you again."

"You won't," he replied, reaching for her. "Because I love you, too, and I'm never letting you go."

She smiled at him in the darkness before kissing him, her lips claiming his and pressing upon him the weight of her emotions, her need for him. And he kissed her back, returning his love and accepting her need, giving of his own.

When they joined together it was with a gentleness and promise they'd never allowed themselves before. Gone was the urgency. Gone was the desperation. Instead, in their place was a solid affirmation of constancy. And as they moved together, climbing the rungs of passion, their movements became a promise—of intention, of love, of stability and the future.

Afterward, they slept together, legs entwined, arms around each other, hearts beating in total sync.

* * *

Valentin's mobile phone woke them as the gray of morning slid through the bedroom window. He and Imogene sprang apart and he felt his heart race with fear as he leaped from the bed and grabbed his trousers from the floor to find the phone. It was the hospital.

"Hello," he said, his heart hammering in his chest. Was it good news, or bad?

"Dr. Horvath. Sorry to call you so early but we wanted to inform you that your grandmother has been scheduled for surgery midafternoon."

"That's great."

"Well, yes," the woman on the other end said before pausing. "But we're having a small issue."

"Issue?"

"She refuses to sign the consent forms unless she sees you and your wife first."

"But why?"

"She hasn't seen fit to inform us of that, sir."

Valentin heard the note of irritation in the woman's voice. "I'm sorry. She's always been strong-minded."

"Well, strong-minded or not, she needs that operation today. Can I take it you'll be in to see her so we can get her to surgery on time? I'm sure I don't need to impress upon you the urgency in her case."

"We'll be there as soon as we can." He ended the call and turned to Imogene. "I'm sorry, we have to go into the hospital. Nagy is asking for us."

"Of course," Imogene said, slipping from the bed

and into a robe. "I'll put the coffee on while you shower. Do you want anything to eat before we go?"

"A slice of toast, maybe?"

"I'm on it. Now, go shower," she said, shooing him in the direction of their bathroom.

He hesitated.

"Are you okay?" Imogene asked, moving to his side quickly.

He wrapped his arms around her and kissed her hard. "I'm glad you're here," he said before kissing her again.

"She'll pull through this, Valentin. They're going to look after her."

She gave him a small smile, then hurried from the room. By the time he was showered she had a light breakfast and coffee ready. She was nowhere to be seen and he assumed she'd gone to shower in her old bathroom. He realized he was right on the money when she reentered the kitchen, ready to leave.

"I've never known a woman to get ready as quickly as you do," he said, his eyes roaming her appreciatively.

"As someone who has always loved her sleep, it was a matter of necessity. Otherwise, I'd arrive everywhere looking like a hag."

"Hag? Impossible, but I appreciate it. Shall we go?"

"Yes, I called Anton. He'll be waiting downstairs. I thought it would be easier than using a cab."

"Good thinking."

When Anton dropped them off at the hospital they went straight up to the ICU. A nurse at the station directed them to Alice's room. The tension gripping Valentin's body eased when he saw his grandmother propped up in her bed. Yes, she was still seriously ill, but there was a fire in her eyes that he recognized immediately.

"You took your time."

Her voice was weak but he heard the indomitable spirit that underpinned everything that Alice Horvath was and every decision she'd made her entire life.

"We're here now," he replied, choosing not to point out that it was still ridiculously early. "How about you tell us what you need to say so you can get better again."

She snorted inelegantly. "Better. There's nothing wrong with me that some good news wouldn't cure. Have you got some good news for me?" Alice looked from one of them to the other. "Well?"

"If you mean have we sorted things out after last night," Imogene said, coming forward and gently taking his grandmother's hand, "then, yes, we have."

"And that woman? Did you get rid of her?"

Valentin bit back the instinctive urge to defend Carla. After all, he'd worked with her for a long time, both here and in Africa. But, he reminded himself, she didn't deserve his loyalty. She'd done her level best to drive his only love away from him. Not once, but twice.

"Yes, she's gone," he said simply.

Alice looked at him. "She's not pregnant, is she?"

"If she is, it certainly isn't my child," he reassured her.

"Last night, when I saw her home, Carla admitted to me that she lied about being pregnant," Imogene informed them both.

"Good." Alice nodded, then turned her gaze back on Imogene. "And you, you've decided to stay with this grandson of mine?"

"Since I'm lucky enough that he can forgive me for believing someone else over him, yes, I am."

"Good," she said again.

"Nagy, stop beating around the bush. What is it that you wanted to tell us?" Valentin pressed.

"I'm not beating around the bush at all, I'm merely ascertaining what the situation is between you two today. I trust you are both equally invested in your marriage now?"

Valentin and Imogene exchanged a glance and in her eyes he could see her love for him reflected clearly.

"Yes, we are," he said firmly.

Alice drew in a deep breath. "Thank goodness, because what I have to tell you two may come as a shock."

That got both their attention.

"In fact," Alice continued, her voice getting stronger now. "One day you might even see the humor in

the situation. All I can say is that it was a good thing neither of you married anyone else after Africa."

"And why not?" Valentin pressed.

"Because it would have been bigamy."

Imogene gasped in shock. "Bigamy? But how? I signed the divorce papers. My lawyer was instructed to send them to Valentin immediately and to file them appropriately on their return."

"I signed the papers. Against my better judgment, I have to say. But I did it because it was clear to me that you wanted out. I sent them back to your lawyer immediately." Valentin looked at his grandmother. "Get to the point, Nagy. Why would it have been bigamy when we did everything we needed to?"

"The papers were never filed," she said with a smile of genuine satisfaction on her pale face. "I'm only sorry it's taken this long to get confirmation of it. We instigated an investigation before your marriage but with communication between the two countries being slow, at best, we decided to take the risk of going ahead before we got confirmation back from Africa. You were both convinced you were free to marry again and, since you were marrying each other, I didn't see the harm.

"Imogene's lawyer was apparently involved in several fraudulent activities with a local warlord. Once that was discovered he was shut down. It seems several local businessmen were angered by his involvement and before another law firm could retrieve the active files being held at his office, the building

was firebombed and burned to the ground. All client information and documents were destroyed."

She looked tired now, but relieved she'd finally managed to tell them the news.

"You mean to say we've been married all along?" Imogene asked incredulously.

"Just think of the Port Ludlow ceremony as an affirmation of your vows," Alice said, her voice growing weaker again.

"You know what this means?" Valentin said, reaching for Imogene's hand and raising it to his mouth to kiss her knuckles. "We get to celebrate two anniversaries."

"For the rest of our lives," Imogene affirmed and reached up to kiss him.

Alice lay in her bed and looked at the happy couple standing beside her and smiled. Not everyone would agree she'd done the right thing pairing them, but she knew, to the depths of her soul, that they belonged together. Always had, always would. They hadn't had the smoothest path to their current happiness but she knew herself that sometimes the hardest road led to the greatest joys. And now that whatever troubles had kept these two apart had been resolved, it had only served to make them stronger than before.

"Mrs. Horvath? Are you ready to sign the consent forms now?"

There was that dratted woman again with her blasted clipboard. "If I must," she acceded.

"Nagy, you must. We want you better again. You still have Galen's wedding to plan," Valentin reminded her as he bent to kiss her on the cheek.

A smile crept across Alice's face. Yes, thank heavens for Galen. He would be her focus now. She could go into this operation, no matter how much it terrified her, secure in the knowledge that she'd effected yet another successful match made in marriage. And when she was well again—and after she was done with Galen—she had plenty more grandchildren to take care of.

Everyone deserved happiness. Everyone deserved a lifetime of love. And it was up to her to make sure they had it.

* * * * *

If you loved Valentin and Imogene, don't miss Galen's story by USA TODAY *bestselling author Yvonne Lindsay.*

Available April 2019 from Harlequin Desire.

#2641 LONE STAR REUNION
Texas Cattleman's Club: Bachelor Auction
by Joss Wood
From feuding families, rancher Daniel Clayton and Alexis Slade have been star-crossed lovers for years. But now the stakes are higher—Alexis ended it even though she's pregnant! When they're stranded together in paradise, it may be their last chance to finally make things right...

#2642 SEDUCTION ON HIS TERMS
Billionaires and Babies • by Sarah M. Anderson
Aloof, rich, gorgeous—that's Dr. Robert Wyatt. The only person he connects with is bartender Jeannie Kaufman. But when Jeannie leaves her job to care for her infant niece, he'll offer her everything she wants just to bring her back into his life...except for his heart.

#2643 BEST FRIENDS, SECRET LOVERS
The Bachelor Pact • by Jessica Lemmon
Flynn Parker and Sabrina Douglas are best friends, coworkers and temporary roommates. He's becoming the hardened businessman he never wanted to be, but her plans to run interference did *not* include an accidental kiss that ignites the heat that has simmered between them for years...

#2644 THE SECRET TWIN
Alaskan Oil Barons • by Catherine Mann
When CEO Ward Benally catches back-from-the-dead Breanna Steele snooping, he'll do anything to protect the company—even convince her to play the role of his girlfriend. But when the sparks between them are real, will she end up in his bed...and in his heart?

#2645 REVENGE WITH BENEFITS
Sweet Tea and Scandal • by Cat Schield
Zoe Alston is ready to make good on her revenge pact, but wealthy Charleston businessman Ryan Dailey defies everything she once believed about him. As their chemistry heats up the sultry Southern nights, will her secrets destroy the most unexpected alliance of all?

#2646 A CONVENIENT SCANDAL
Plunder Cove • by Kimberley Troutte
When critic Jeff Harper's career implodes due to scandal, he does what he vowed never to do—return to Plunder Cove. There, he'll have his family's new hotel—*if* he marries for stability...and avoids the temptation of the gorgeous chef vying to be his hotel's next star.

SPECIAL EXCERPT FROM

HARLEQUIN®
Desire

*Flynn Parker and Sabrina Douglas are best friends,
coworkers and temporary roommates. He's becoming
the hardened businessman he never wanted to be,
but her plans to run interference did not include an
accidental kiss that ignites the heat that's simmered
between them for years…*

Read on for a sneak peek of
Best Friends, Secret Lovers *by Jessica Lemmon,
part of her Bachelor Pact series!*

They'd never talked about how they were always overlapping
each other with dating other people.

It was an odd thing to notice.

Why had Sabrina noticed?

Sabrina Douglas was his best girl friend. Girl, space,
friend. But Flynn felt a definite stir in his gut.

For the first time in his life, sex wasn't off the table for
him and Sabrina.

Which meant he needed his head examined.

After the tasting, Sabrina chattered about her favorite
cheeses and how she couldn't believe they didn't serve wine
at the tour.

"What kind of establishment doesn't offer you wine with
cheese?" she exclaimed as they strolled down the boardwalk.
Which gave him a great view of her ass—another part of her
he'd noticed before, but not like he was noticing now.

Not helping matters was the fact that he didn't have to wonder what kind of underwear she wore beneath that tight denim. He knew.

They'd been friends and comfortable around each other for long enough that no amount of trying to forget would erase the image of her wearing a black thong that perfectly split those cheeks into two biteable orbs.

"What do you think?" She spun and faced him, the wind kicking her hair forward, a few strands sticking to her lip gloss. He reached her in two steps. Before he thought it through, he swept those strands away, ran his fingers down her cheek and tipped her chin, his head a riot of bad ideas.

With a deep swallow, he called up ironclad Parker willpower and stopped touching his best friend. "I think you're right."

His voice was as rough as gravel.

"You're distracted. Are you thinking about work?"

"Yes," he lied through his teeth.

"You're going to have to let it go at some point. Give in to the urge." She drew out the word *urge*, perfectly pursing her lips and leaning forward with a playful twinkle in her eyes that would tempt any mortal man to sin.

And since Flynn was nothing less than mortal, he palmed the back of her head and pressed his mouth to hers.

Don't miss what happens next!
Best Friends, Secret Lovers by Jessica Lemmon,
part of her Bachelor Pact series!

Available February 2019 wherever
Harlequin® Desire books and ebooks are sold.

www.Harlequin.com

Want to give in to temptation with
steamy tales of irresistible desire?

Check out **Harlequin® Presents®**,
Harlequin® Desire and
Harlequin® Kimani™ Romance books!

New books available every month!

CONNECT WITH US AT:

Facebook.com/groups/HarlequinConnection

Facebook.com/HarlequinBooks

Twitter.com/HarlequinBooks

Instagram.com/HarlequinBooks

Pinterest.com/HarlequinBooks

ReaderService.com

H HARLEQUIN®

**ROMANCE WHEN
YOU NEED IT**

PGENRE2018